Wes was ba... a yard ......
rifle shot came at his second step and plowed
dirt six inches from his foot.

"Don't move again or you're one dead line
rider," a voice called out from the brush next
to a nearby stack of pines. "We got three rifles
on you, boy. Get down on your knees, now!"

Wes went down on his knees. Two men rode
out of the brush just then, both with rifles
aimed at him.

Taking a big chance, Wes dove to the side,
rolled and scrambled to the door of the shack.

Two shots scratched the ground around him,
but missed.

Inside, he grabbed his Spencer, leaned out
and sent a round in the riders' direction. They
turned tail for cover.

Wes found the rest of the ammunition for the
Spencer and took up a spot between the door
and the window.

Something told him it was going to be a long
night.

LINE RIDER'S REVENGE

Chet Cunningham

PINNACLE BOOKS
WINDSOR PUBLISHING CORP.

PINNACLE BOOKS are published by

Windsor Publishing Corp.
475 Park Avenue South
New York, NY 10016

The P logo Reg U.S. Pat & TM off. Pinnacle is a trademark
of Windsor Publishing Corp.

First Printing: January, 1994

Printed in the United States of America

One

Wes Parker looked up from where he was working a long splice into his lariat to form a new end loop and saw Old Jed riding into the ranch yard on his limping roan mare. Old Jed was supposed to be up in the high lonely on Line Shack Twelve. That was the farthest out line shack in the whole massive Bar-N cattle spread.

A coyote-sized, brown dog trotted alongside the mare, never moving more than a few feet ahead or behind. Old Jed rode his mount to the near side of the corral, and that was when Wes knew the old man was in trouble. He didn't step down from the saddle on the left side. Instead he brought his right leg over the horse's rump, turned on his stomach and slid down the side of the mare slowly until his right foot touched the ground.

Wes left the leather shop and hurried out to the corral. Old Jed had tied his dark red mare to a rail, patted his dog and sent it to the horse trough for a drink.

The line rider leaned on the corral and slumped down against the lower railing and sat down on the ground. A scowl on his face masked the pain Wes figured Jed must be feeling. Wes saw him wince when he put any pressure at all on his left leg.

Wes had known Old Jed since the day he signed on at the Bar-N. He was crotchety, argued about everything and spent most of his time in line shacks as far from the ranch as possible.

His face was dull brown from the wind and sun. His black hat slid to one side showing the "cowboy" suntan line just above the eyes where his Stetson had covered his head and left it a pasty white. His green eyes were dull, and Old Jed gave a long sigh as he straightened his left leg and let it down gently on the ground.

"Jed. What the hell you doing down from Twelve?" Wes asked as he knelt beside the old man in the powder-fine Montana summer dust.

"I'm about used up, boy. Wes, ain't it? Cain't see a damn thing out of my left eye no more. Big cloud rolled over it, and I can't see diddly cow piss on a bright sunny day."

"What about your leg?"

The old man wheezed and reached down and massaged his knee tenderly. "Damn knee joint is out of whack, and I got me a hurt the size of a baseball on my calf. Don't know what the hell is happening to me."

Wes looked around as Caleb Norton hurried

6

up. Caleb owned the Bar-N Ranch. He walked with legs slightly bowed after forty years in the saddle. He was sixty-two, cowhide tough and as quick as a rattler on a hot day. He knelt down in the dust and stared at his longtime rider.

"Jed, what happened?"

Jed told him about his ails. "Caleb, I said I'd do the high lonely long as I could. Figure now's the time I'm through up there. Can't do the job needs done on Twelve. Me and Pochuck here both on our last legs." The mangy mutt had returned and sat down beside Jed, wagging his long tail and lying so his muzzle rested on the old cowhand's thigh.

"Nonsense, Jed," Caleb told him. "You're tired and just feeling down for a bit. We'll have you up and around in no time. We'll get you to town to see old Doc Braithwaite. You and Pochuck deserve a rest. Wes, give me a hand. We'll get Jed into the end bedroom up at the ranch house."

"Bunkhouse always been good enough for me," Jed said. "It'll do me fine right now."

Caleb ignored the mild protest, and he and Wes lifted the old man and carried him fifty yards up the slope to where the two-story ranch house stood. They maneuvered through the kitchen door and into the second room down and sat him on the edge of the bed with its soft red spread.

Old Jed grinned through his gray, scraggly beard. "Damn, ain't had me a mattress like this for a long time."

Caleb eased off the rider's boots and lifted the left blue jeans pants leg. The swelling on his calf was a two-inch high knot of ugly purple and black with red stabbing out from it up and down.

"You just rest easy, Jed," Caleb said. "I'll have the cook work up some food for you."

Old Jed's green eyes brightened and he nodded. "Sounds good. I hate to put you out none, but would there be any coffee? I ran out about a month ago, and . . ."

"Whole damn pot of coffee coming up, Jed. Now you settle back. That leg don't look good. I'm sending a man into town right now to bring out Doc Braithwaite. He ain't so busy he can't come out this once."

Wes left the bedroom and went out to take care of the horse. It had a bad left front foot, but a new shoe and some rest should make it well. He took off the sun-browned saddle and hung it on a peg in the small barn and turned the horse over to their farrier.

Line riding. He'd served one summer on a line shack with another outfit in Kansas. It wasn't quite so high or so lonely in Kansas, but it was a three-month stay in the back country with only two visitors all summer. He'd thought about it since. The high lonely job had its good points.

He went back to finishing the long splice in his lariat and had it done, the ends clipped off and burned-in, when he got word from one of the cowhands that the boss wanted to see him in the office.

On the Bar-N, the office was in a red-painted building attached to the back of the ranch house. It held just two rooms, a big one where Caleb Norton had a desk and some files and records, and a smaller room where Caleb slept when he didn't want to take the time to go to the master bedroom.

Wes knocked on the inner door, and Caleb looked up.

"Parker, come in. As you know, we have ourselves a small problem. Didn't I hear once that you did some line riding work?"

"Did one summer down in Kansas, yes, sir."

"Like it?"

"Well, it's different. Lonely out there. Leastwise it was straight cowhand work. No fence making or fixing barns and such."

Caleb grinned. "Never could figure out why a cowboy can't fix a fence, but been a long time since I did my whole day on the back of a cow pony." Caleb looked at Wes like he was a prime steer ready for market.

"How old are you, Wes?"

"Twenty-one right now. Just had a birthday."

"So now you can legally drink and gamble and even vote."

"I reckon, if them chances comes up."

"I've noticed you don't go into town much on Saturday nights."

"No, sir. Too long a ride just for a little fun."

"You can read and write, Parker?"

9

"Yes, sir. Made it through grade eight before I went to doing ranch work."

"Good. Parker, I want you to take over Line Shack Twelve."

"Way out there? That's the farthest out one we have, Mr. Norton. To hell and gone up there in the breaks."

"True, nigh into Canada. Leastwise you won't have no foreman ramrodding you around."

"Yeah, but I'll have to do my own cooking."

"You did that before down in Kansas."

"Just hadn't figured. . . ."

"How long you been riding for me, Wes?"

"Over two years now, Mr. Norton."

"I kept you on over the winter when I could have laid you off, right?"

"Yes, sir. I appreciate that."

"Well, Wes, now it's time to return the favor. I want you on Twelve. I don't want any big argument. I just argue with cattle buyers, vets and a woman now and then. You'll get a resupply every two months, won't have to put up with any other boss. When your work is done up there, you can kick your heels up on a stump and enjoy the purple sunsets in the high country.

"Also, you'll be making an extra ten dollars a month. No time for argument. I want you to go over and talk with Old Jed. Find out everything he can tell you about Twelve. Each line shack has a little different country around it. Find out what you need to know about the work up there, any problems he's having, what's been going on. Take the rest of the day.

10

"First thing tomorrow morning we'll have a packhorse all loaded for you, and you'll be on your way."

Wes looked up at his boss. Caleb Norton didn't like arguments. Wes knew if he didn't go up to Twelve, he might be on his horse riding away from the Bar-N looking for a new job. He wrinkled his brow a moment, then took a long breath and let it out.

Might not be so bad up on the high lonely. Maybe six months more, then he'd be back for the winter rest. Hell yes, he better give it a try.

"Yes, sir. I'll go up to Twelve for you, Mr. Norton. So now I best have that talk with Old Jed. Oh, do you have a tablet or something I can use to write down what he tells me? I'll need a new notebook or a pad, too, to keep my log in when I'm up there. For the cattle count and all."

Caleb grinned and handed Wes two tablets and four yellow wooden lead pencils. "These should get you started. Get your gear together and figure what you want to take with you and what to leave here. You can store your stuff in the back room of the bunkhouse."

The ranch owner paused and scowled and stared at Wes a minute. "One more thing, Wes. That leg wound on Jed, looks almighty like an infected and festered up gunshot wound to me with the lead still inside. Wonder it ain't killed the old man. Would have me.

"You find out how he got it. Something strange must be going on up around Twelve.

11

Ain't heard of nothing, but you quiz Jed. He probably wouldn't tell me. Ask him what to watch out for."

Wes gulped. Old Jed shot? Now the man tells him. Damn. He bobbed his head, held the tablets tight and left the office.

A few minutes later, Old Jed looked at Wes with a sly grin.

"Damn but they got a good cook here. Ate so much I damn near bust my britches. Jeez, Wes. Good food all fixed, a soft mattress with no damn bedbugs, soap and hot water, clean towels, pretty green curtains, all the comforts of home." He stopped and watched Wes using a penknife to shave a sharp point on a new wooden pencil.

"Uh, oh. Looks like you got nailed to go up and take my place, right?"

"About the way I reacted to my big chance, Jed."

"Good, you'll do fine up there. First off, you know where it is?"

"Farthest out line shack we have. As I remember, it's about ten miles north of the end of the Willow River, just down from Whitlash Buttes. There's a series of low hills rising out of the plateau and some rougher breaks to the west. Somebody said it was five miles from the Canadian border and more than twenty-five miles from the ranch house."

"Closer to thirty miles. You don't get no help from another line rider. There's one eight miles to the east and south a ways, but that's Larry Rawls, and it's past some real rugged breaks and canyons in there. Larry's a mean son-of-a-bitch who ain't never helped nobody in his life. Stay a mile and a half away from that no good jackass."

Wes chuckled. "I'd guess you and him ain't the best of buddies."

"True." Old Jed sipped at his black coffee. Then he poured his cup full from a metal pot that sat on a small table near the bed.

"Hear you been in the high country before."

"One summer, down in Kansas."

"Kansas? Hell, no part of Kansas is as bad as any part of Montana. This is really high. Figure the line shack is at about thirty-four or thirty-five hundred feet up on this big plateau. Summer comes late, and winter slams in to live up there early. You know the work a line rider's got to do."

"Give me a list. Maybe I forgot some of it."

"Heeeeeeerah. Not so. Once a line rider, you never forget what you got to do. First you protect them critters from thieves and cougars and wolves. That's the big one. Ain't had no rustling up there to speak of. No place to take the animals north. Not much sense in moving anything to the west. Got the big Slash S over there, and they protect their own pretty damn good.

"So any rustling would have to come from the south and right through the close in ranges. Line riders down there got more worry that way than you do."

He sipped the coffee, then took another bite from one of a pair of caramel cinnamon rolls

13

on a plate on the bed next to him. "I dreamed of rolls like these.

"The tally. You keep a tally on the critters whenever you ride the fence. Course, riding the fence ain't but a way of talking. We ain't got no fences up there, but there is a kind of a trail that swings around the north-most section where we got any beef. You'll find it easy enough. I made out a map and left it on the shack table."

"What about the doctoring?" Wes asked. "Much of that?"

"Not a lot you can do. Lop ear now and then and a few cows get black leg or lump jaw. Just do like it says on the cans of salve, and that's about it. If a critter gets sick and is gonna die, no way you can stop it. Just mark it down on your tally and what you think the cause was and dig the body under the ground."

"The roundup comes near to Twelve, as I remember," Wes said. "Gonna be late this year, so they might get up there in a couple of weeks, maybe three from what the talk is."

"Yep, you get to eat off the chuck wagon then. That's about all there is to it. Ride that top trail every week or so and keep a tally and watch for sick and down animals."

"Jed, that leg of yours, it's a bullet wound, ain't it? Infected, about to drive you crazy?"

Jed looked up and nodded slowly.

"If'n I'm going up there, you got to tell who shot you and why. I got to know. Something strange going on up in the north range? Is there a crazy hermit up there or a rawhider, what?"

14

Old Jed sighed, winced when he moved. "Wish that sawbones would get here. Damn, that hurts." He looked at Wes. "Oh, damn. Thought maybe it would go away. Didn't tell Caleb, but I guess I got to. You deserve to know, you goin' up there an' all."

He sighed again. "Happened over a week ago. I know, I know a bullet got to come out. But no mind. I was riding on the west side, not seeing too good out of one eye and hurting on my knee. I got down to rest my roan, and some Jasper lifted up from in back of some brush and shot me.

"I got out my Colt and peppered all six rounds into the brush and then used my Remington repeater and shot into it as I hobbled back out of six-gun range. Never did see nobody. He didn't say word one. Just started whaling away at me. Shot three times, hit my leg with one."

He tried to roll over and groaned and lay back. "So I told you."

"Where was it, Jed. Exactly?"

"Don't know, boy. Maybe five, six miles to the west of the shack. Where some of them first breaks come and those little ridges and valleys. A mess cleaning them out of cattle come roundup. In that area. Couldn't find the exact spot again myself."

He sighed and closed his eyes. "Now, boy, I told you. You can tell Caleb. Me, I got me some sleep to catch up on. Put that other roll on the stand. I'll shut my old eyes and let them rest.

15

Leastwise let one of them rest. The other damned eyeball ain't done no real work for two weeks now."

Wes moved the plate with the roll on it, then paused at the door. He was about to wish the old cowboy good night when he saw that his eyes were already closed, and his breathing was soft and even.

By that time, it was nearly three in the afternoon. Wes went to the bunkhouse and looked at his gear. He had made a three-foot long box from cut lumber and put it at the end of his bunk. In it he had stored his few treasures, some clothes, a packet of pictures and a few letters from home. He'd have to decide what to take and what to leave. All the time he thought about Old Jed getting shot. He'd have to tell Mr. Norton. He wondered if he would still go up.

Wes went to Caleb's office and repeated what Old Jed had told him.

"Damnation! Somebody is cooking up something. How in hell they gonna rustle any stock from that area? Dumb. Must have some kind of a plan. They must have shot at Jed just to warn him, hit him by mistake."

"I'm still going up there, Mr. Norton?"

"Damn right. Need you more than ever now. You're warned. You can look for them, watch for anybody not supposed to be on that range."

"I'm no range detective, Mr. Norton."

"Me either, but we protect what's ours. Your job is to protect those cattle up there. Now finish getting ready to move out."

By chow time Wes had decided what gear to take and leave. The clothes, extra six-gun, his second pair of work boots and other essentials, he put his gear in a carpetbag that he'd tie to the back of his saddle or the packhorse in the morning. That decided, he took the wooden box into the store room at the back of the bunkhouse and snapped a little padlock on the hasp.

Padlocks like that were just to keep the honest folks out of his things. A real thief wouldn't let a twenty-cent padlock stop him. Next he went over to the kitchen and asked the cook if they were putting together his supplies for Line Shack Twelve.

They were all ready to go. He had three gunny sacks full of staples, as well as some slabs of bacon and a ham and a few other items that wouldn't keep all that long in the summer heat.

"Eat up the good stuff first, and then work down to the beans and dried fruit," the cook said. He was a middle-aged black man who was the best range cook Wes had ever seen. He had frizzy gray hair now in tight little rings on his head, a sagging face with big brown eyes that could charm the eggs right out of the chickens. His pot belly rolled when he walked, but it never seemed to get in his way.

"I'll bring up some more grub for you when we do the roundup in your area. Save you a trip down that way."

At the chow hall that night, the men knew Wes had drawn the high lonely duty and some of them razzed him about it.

"Hell, Wes, you'll be skinny as a cut-ear, hard-feeding steer by the time we get up there on the roundup," one cowhand called.

Roach Logan, the Bar-N ramrod, lit a just-rolled cigarette and shook his head. "Hell, Wes, you're going up there to easy duty. Even so, within a week you'll wish you was back down here where the food is all cooked and waiting for you. The secret up there is to relax and take it easy. Don't take your guarding job too seriously. Pretend it's a vacation, and you'll get along fine."

Logan started to say something else, but two other men yelled at Wes, asking for a loan. Everyone knew that a line shack man on a high lonely post got ten dollars a month more pay.

The next morning at daylight, Wes readied for his northward trip. He had thirty miles or a bit more to travel. He would ride his favorite cow pony, Matilda. She was a veteran of two trail drives and countless roundups. She had one ear with a bite out of it from an amorous stallion and had retaliated with a solid kick in the stud's midsection. She was a true sorrel, reddish brown in color with an almost pure white mane and tail. He'd had her for three years, ever since he got into the West and started learning to be a cow hand.

The last thing Caleb told Wes that morning before he left was to keep his eyes open. "Jed just might have tangled with a goddamned rawhider. You know what they are, Wes? Usually a family of sorts that roams the plains and ranches. They'll kill a man for his horse and saddle. They raid small farms, rape the women, then kill everyone there, steal everything they can sell in the next town and kill all the animals and burn down the buildings.

"Usually they're dirty as sin and wear rags for clothes. Watch out for them bastards. Might be that old Jed chanced on one, and he shot first the way they always do. Be watchful."

Yeah, Wes thought about it again now as he looked at the packhorse. She wasn't much. He figured she was living out her days in that low packhorse profession after a good eight years of glory as a top cutting horse. He had tied his carpetbag on the top of the sacks of food and supplies, pushed his best Colt revolver into brown leather on his right hip and mounted up.

For the first five miles he traveled familiar territory, then he angled up a gentle valley and over a small ridge, and he was into an area of the ranch that technically Caleb Norton didn't "own" in a legal sense. However, they held the use of the land with men, horses and weapons. It was the typical set-up for controlling large sections of land. The ranchers did it by homesteading the best source of water in a given area. In this case it was the Little Chino River.

Caleb Norton had homesteaded a strip of land on both sides of the river. His claim was only a hundred yards wide and straddled the river. The narrow pieces of the claim might be a half-mile long, or fifty yards long or a mile long, depending on how many twists and turns the river took. By the time he had used up his 180 acres of homestead in these hundred-yard wide strips along the stream, he had staked out land covering nearly five miles of the Little Chino River.

He had a brother and four ranch hands stake claims they later sold to him for a dollar each. These were the same kind of jiggled pattern along the Little Chino and tied up the river for twenty miles.

Land in Montana without water is worthless to farm or run cattle on, and Norton had "inherited" the rights to hundreds of thousands of acres of grazing land that drained into the Little Chino River by right of use.

As mile after mile melted away under the slow plodding of the two horses, Wes decided that Montana in the summer wasn't a hell of a lot better than Montana in the winter. Now spring, there was a fine three weeks.

He came over a small rise and glanced behind him at the downslope. A half mile back he saw a rider moving in the same direction he was over the part brown, part green prairie. Curious. Nobody should be out in this area. At once he wondered if this was the same man who had shot Old Jed. Wes rode down the slope and came to a small feeder stream that watered a quarter section of graze and sprouted a thin ribbon of green and some willow brush.

Wes looked back, saw that the other rider hadn't topped the rise yet, so he turned and rode into the brush until both his animals were concealed. Then he pulled the Spencer repeating rifle from the boot of the saddle and levered a round into the chamber. He had six more cartridges in the magazine tube that went through the stock. He also had five more loaded tubes in his gear.

For five minutes he waited, but the rider he thought had been following him never came over the top of the rise. He waited another twenty minutes by his pocket watch. When no one showed over the hill, he stepped into his saddle and walked his animals north again. He'd follow this trickle of water uphill until it ended and then angle over the next small rise and head due north toward the jagged hills and bluffs that were called the Whitlash Buttes.

Now and again he'd turn in his saddle and check his back trail. Once he thought he saw movement a quarter of a mile behind him, but as he continued to watch that spot, he couldn't be sure. He stopped under a pair of spring-green cottonwoods beside a dry streambed and ate the two sandwiches the cook had fixed for him. Nobody rode up on him so he kicked out onto the trail after ten minutes.

About two hours later, he came down a slope to a small creek and pushed into the brush just to make another back trail check. This time a rider came over the rise behind at a trot, then scanned the space ahead. Wes figured the rider didn't see the horses he was following. He dropped the horse to a walk. He must not have meant to be caught in the open, but he knew he was and came forward at an easy pace.

Nobody but a Bar-N ranch hand had any business in this section of the range. So who was the stranger riding toward him? Maybe the rawhider who shot Old Jed, waiting for him to come back.

Wes stepped down from Matilda, rifle in hand, and went to the fringes of the brush so he could see the man riding forward but still remain hidden. Best to see who the gent was. He might be on legitimate business up in here, but Wes couldn't think what it might be.

When the rider was thirty feet from the brush, Wes stepped out with his rifle aimed at the man.

"Hold it right there, stranger. Slide down on this side of your horse and keep your hands in plain sight. Who are you and what are you doing on Bar-N range?"

The man in a tan shirt grinned. "Bar-N? Hell, I'm looking for the Slant S. Ain't it around here somewhere?"

"You've missed it by forty miles. Who owns the Slant S?" The other man cleared his horse and let his hands move slowly down to his sides. He grinned and chuckled.

"Hell, I don't know. Looking for work. Told me in town it was out this way." Wes almost bought it. Only the man had a week's growth of whiskers, his clothes were sweat-stained and dirty as sin. Was this guy a rawhider? His hogleg at his right hip was tied low and the leather polished and clean. Not a rawhider, a gunsharp.

"Guess I'll just have to mount up and be on

my way. Which direction do I take to find this Slash S outfit? I need a riding job."

Wes didn't take his hands off the rifle to point. "Turn due west for about ten miles. Find the Bachelor River and follow upstream for twelve miles, and somebody can tell you how to find the Slant S."

The gunsharp touched his brown hat with his left hand and started to turn toward his horse. Instead his right hand ripped his six-gun out of leather and angled the weapon up to shoot just as Wes fired the rifle.

The two gunshots blasted into the silent Montana back country almost at the same time.

Two

Wes heard the sharp report of his own rifle, and almost at the same time sensed the blast from the six-gun and the flash of light. Before he could move or even think, something smashed into his upper left arm and spun him half around.

He'd been shot!

His first thought was to look at his wound, then he concentrated on staring at the other man. All this happened in a fraction of a second, and he saw the stranger take the rifle round in his chest and slam backwards two steps. Then the man cried out and dropped the revolver and crumpled to his knees. His eyes showed the whites, and he crashed forward on his face in the dusty Montana high plateau. He never moved again.

Wes swallowed hard and levered a new round into his Spencer with his right hand. His arm burned like a dozen branding irons were on it. He held the Spencer up to cover the man as he walked around so he could see the stranger's face. It lay in powdery dust. His nose was completely covered by the dust, and no breath came from it to disturb the soil.

Wes stepped closer and pushed away the six-gun, shoving it gently with his toe so it wouldn't discharge again. Then he tipped the body over on its back.

A growing pool of blood showed on the man's chest, soaking through his shirt. His eyes stared lifeless at the hot afternoon sun.

"Christ a'mighty!" Wes whispered. He'd just killed this man. Yes, he'd killed one man before, a man who deserved to die. This one had tried to kill him. He would have if Wes hadn't had his rifle ready and aimed at him. As it happened, only a hundredth of a second had made the difference, had saved his life. The gunsharp had needed about that much more time to get his aim accurate before he pulled the trigger.

Was this the man who shot Old Jed from ambush? He might have been. If so, the threat of a gunman up here was over. Or was it? A man like this wouldn't shoot five times from ambush just to scare a man. He'd walk up to him, outdraw him, kill him and laugh as he rode away. Wes had seen more than one gunsharp.

He bent and picked up the six-gun, a fancy Remington with pearl handles. It was one of the expensive models. He pushed it in his belt. He didn't like to, but he figured he had to go through the dead man's pockets. He took personal papers, a small purse holding four dollars, a jackknife and two Civil War medals from the Rebels. A letter in his shirt pocket was addressed to J. L. Liberty, General Delivery, Great Falls, Montana Territory.

Wes looked at the sun. He didn't have time to bury the man, didn't even have a shovel. The buzzards and coyotes would take care of him in no time. He'd send the man's effects back to his family if the letter gave any return address. At least they should know he was dead.

Wes caught the reins of the man's horse and led it over to his two and tied it with a short lead rope to the pack animal's pannier. He mounted up, took one more look at the gun-sharp, then rode on north, heading straight for the Whitlash Buttes far ahead. He figured he had about another ten miles to ride.

His arm hurt again, and he looked at it. Blood on the shirtsleeve, and now he could feel it running down his arm to his elbow. He rolled up that sleeve and saw the wound down about six inches from his shoulder.

The hot .45 slug had nipped his upper arm, gouged out a half-inch groove and plowed on through not slowing down for skin, shirt or muscle. He bled like a stuck shoat. Wes pulled his oversize bandanna, from around his neck and lapped it over the wound, then wrapped it around his arm, pulling the cloth tight.

He used his teeth and right hand to tear the corner of the bandanna, making an eight-inch split so he could part the halves and put them

26

around his arm and hopefully tie the ends in the front.

With two hands, it was a five second job. This way, using his right hand and his teeth, it took him a mile to get the bandanna ends knotted even loosely. He brought his shirtsleeve down, figuring that would help hold the bandage in place.

He had seen Bar-N cattle along the way. They tended to group around small sinks and feeder streams that wound their way toward the river. Now for a spell he saw no cattle and realized the land was lifting as he rode. He was going higher and higher on the gradual slope of the plateau that swept down from the great Rocky Mountains far to the west.

The grass was shorter here, there was less of it and few watering holes.

He thought about the dead man again. He couldn't help it. He was sorry he had killed him, but he'd had no choice, he was positive of that. He couldn't be the one who shot Old Jed. If he was, what was he doing way out here? Old Jed was shot five or six miles along the north boundary, not out here in the open. The more he thought of it, the more he figured this man called Liberty wasn't the one who shot Old Jed.

At last he came to the place where he remembered they had staged the roundup in this sector last year. It was a comparatively flat area that at one time must have been an old lake. As he remembered, the line rider's shack was just over a slight rise to the left. He rode that way with

27

his short string of animals behind him and stopped suddenly as he topped the rise.

He saw the shack in the distance, not more than a quarter of a mile off. What halted him was the lazy spiral of smoke coming out of the makeshift chimney. Someone must be inside. He saw no horse. No one stood at the tiny spring in back of the shack in a gully.

Wes tied Matilda to a bit of sage and studied the shack again. If it had any windows, they weren't on this side. He pulled his six-gun and walked forward, eyes alert, watching everything in front and to the sides. It could be a trap. Start a fire in the chimney and then jump him on the way to the cabin.

He ran the last thirty yards, coming to a stop at the back of the shack, which had been made of some saw lumber, logs, old tin and lots of sod for the roof. Wildflowers grew out of the top of the shack. He paused, trying to listen for any sounds.

For a moment he heard a bit of a tune someone sang, then it was gone. Wes edged around the corner of the shack and studied the area. The side wall was eight feet wide. A bucket, an old blanket and some assorted tools lay there. There was no window. He moved up to the corner and peered around toward the front of the building.

Now he saw a horse tied close to the shack. It stood on three legs and had a wild look in its eyes. The animal held its right front leg off the ground. Now and again the horse put the hoof

28

on the ground, shivered evidently with pain and lifted it again.

The front of the shack showed signs of use. A wooden box that looked as if it might be for storage lay against the front wall. A window with four, foot-square panes showed to the left of the door.

A small step had been fashioned of saw boards leading to a door that swung inward and stood open. The singing came again, some little tune with which Wes was not familiar. It died again from lack of words or melody or perhaps both.

Wes held the hammer of his six-gun as he cocked it to muffle the sound, then edged around the wall and stepped through the door and into the shack.

He could see little for a moment, then his eyes adjusted to the dimmer light, and he saw a man in front of the small wood-burning stove working over a half-filled frying pan.

"Don't move," Wes said.

His vision cleared more, and he saw that the person at the stove was a young man, maybe no more than seventeen.

"Hey, easy, easy. You don't need that cannon. Hey, I'm not here to rob anything or hurt you. Just got myself lost and my horse went lame and I saw the shack. This a line shack right? I must be on the Bar-N 'cause over at the Slash S we don't have any line shacks set up this fancy."

Wes lowered the Colt. "Over at the Slash S? Who are you?"

"I'm Tom Swanson."

"Your pa is Zip Swanson, owner of the Slash S?"

"Yep."

"You're a long way from home."

"What I planned. Just didn't figure on getting lost. Where am I?"

"This is Line Shack Twelve, about thirty miles from the Bar-N Ranch buildings."

"Oh boy. I wanted to go east, 'cause I figure Pa wouldn't go look for me this way, but not this far."

"You must be at least thirty miles from your home place."

"Damn. I been doing everything wrong lately."

Wes grinned. "Stir those fried spuds or you're going to burn them, and I'm hungry. You look to have enough fried potatoes there for two."

Wes put away his hogleg. "I'm going to unpack my gear. I've got some bacon we can fry and mix in with the spuds. Old Jed must have run out of bacon a long time ago. I'm new on this post. Old guy who used to be here got all stove up and had a bad leg."

Wes watered the horses where the spring had been dug out to provide a water hole. Then he unloaded the packhorse and stowed the food inside in the big pantry that was almost empty. He took the pannier off and set it next to the side of the shack. It would go back on the next trip to the ranch.

He unsaddled his mount, then the dead

30

man's, and out of curiosity went through the man's saddlebags. He found two more letters and a bank bag. The leather bag was imprinted "Long Grass Territorial Bank." Inside he found two thick packets of bills with paper wrappers around them.

Each packet showed twenty-dollar bills on the outside. No matter what denomination, they were stacks of greenbacks that amounted to a lot of cash. He pushed them back in the saddlebag. The other side of the bag contained a pad and writing paper, three pencils and a large gum eraser. Was the man a bank robber or a writer?

Wes took the saddlebags inside and pushed them both under the bunk in the corner of the shack. He went out and checked the horse with the Slash S brand. The animal had a bad stone bruise on its leg just over the hoof. It would need a week of rest to get back the use of the leg.

Inside, Wes told Tom Swanson about his horse.

"Damn, so what am I supposed to do for a week?"

"Think of some way to make up with your Pa so you can go back home," Wes said.

Tom looked at him quickly, saw he was serious.

"Damn, yeah I guess. I got mad and he got mad and I ran off and he let me go. Maybe if I just went back and told him I was wrong, and

31

I'll learn ranching from the bottom up the way he wants me to."

"What do you really want to do?"

"Be a fiddler like my Uncle Arnie. He's good. Plays at all of the county fairs and has his own little bunch of guys who play at weddings and parties and dances."

"He do anything else or just play fiddle?"

"Sure, he's a butcher in town. He told me you got to be damn lucky or damn good to make a living fiddling. Still, I took lessons from him for four years. I can cut a pretty mean stick with my fiddle."

"Why can't you do both, be a fiddler and a rancher, too?"

Tom grinned, shook his head. "Damn, that's what my pa said. That's when I ran out."

"So far he hasn't accused you of being a horse thief."

Tom laughed. "So far. Looks like these spuds are about done, where's that bacon?"

Turned out that Tom had only arrived at the shack that afternoon. He'd walked the last five miles, nursing the horse along on the way.

"Figured I could rest up here a couple of days, maybe my mare would get use of her foot again."

"I got a spare horse out there," Wes said. "Not the packhorse, the other one. You write me out a bill of sale for one dollar for your horse, and I'll sell you my horse for a dollar with a bill of sale, and we'll be all even and grieven."

"Yeah, sounds good for transportation. Now all I have to do is figure out where to go."

"You bring your fiddle with you?"

Tom lifted his brows. "Nope, didn't take time."

"Looks to me like you figured on going back for it, maybe going back to stay. But it's up to you to decide that. I need to get some things set up here before it gets too dark. We got one lamp or two, or lanterns?"

He found two coal oil lamps and a five-gallon can of coal oil near full. There were two lanterns hanging outside, and both were full of fuel. He aired out the blankets on the bunk for half an hour and figured he'd hang them out all day tomorrow and maybe wash the ones he could.

The bunk was made of saw boards and no mattress. He'd fix that with leaves or straw or weeds or something. He didn't cotton to sleeping on boards for six months.

They had the fried spuds and bacon for supper, along with some baking powder biscuits the cook had packed for him. They put honey on them and boiled coffee and settled back after the meal full and content.

"I been sleeping in the open last two nights, so I been watching the stars," Tom said. "Damn interesting."

It went dark all of a sudden outside, and they walked out and studied the heavens. A pair of coyotes howled at each other in the distance. Wes didn't know if they were just talking, or if it was some kind of a love song and the two would get together. He'd heard the coyotes had a method in their howling.

They sat outside on a log backed against the shack and watched and listened. A short, crisp barking came from somewhere nearby, and Wes listened for it again. It sounded once more but didn't repeat.

"What was that?" Wes asked.

Tom shrugged. "Can't be certain, but it warn't no dog or wolf or coyote. Might have been a red fox. Don't know for sure what kind of a call they have. I saw a full grown red fox sniffing around the shack here today when I rode in. He watched me a minute, then went tearing away past the spring."

"A yep. . . . Didn't know there were any red foxes in Montana."

"They go about wherever they want."

"Listen to that," Wes said.

They both were quiet for a minute.

"Listen to what?"

"The silence, it's great. No foreman screeching at me. Old Caleb not chewing me out for something I did or didn't do. Kind of nice."

They sat for a time watching the moon and the stars. A cloud shunted across the moon, dimming everything for a while. Then it passed, and they could see the spring and the three horses where they had been picketed near the splash of green grass.

Ten minutes of silence turned into a half hour and then an hour.

"Damn, wish I had my fiddle."

"So you're going back in the morning?" Wes asked.

"If'n we can make that trade of horses and sign bills of sale for each other."

"Let's go in and do it right now."

Inside they lit a lamp, and Wes tore off two pages from the tablet he had, and they each wrote out bills of sale to the other, describing the horse and any brands on it. Wes had to go out with a lantern and inspect the dead man's horse but came back and said it was unbranded.

When they were done, they each read the other one's bill of sale, then both signed them as seller and buyer and they grinned.

"Damn, but I know I shouldn't have run off that way. Guess I got to learn some things about a temper. Good to have if you can control it. My pa always said that, but he didn't always and I know I don't always, but I'm trying."

They made motions about getting to bed. Tom waved both hands. "Don't bother about me. I'll just spread out my blanket on the floor here and sleep. Looks about as soft as that wooden mattress you got on the bunk. You gotta make yourself a mat to go in there out of straw or hay or something."

Wes kicked off his boots and put his revolver under a pillow of his shirt and trousers. He was almost asleep when he realized that he hadn't moved those saddlebags with the money in them. He shrugged. He could trust Tom. The kid must be exactly what he seemed to be. But what if he wasn't? A knife through his own heart, and Tom would have two good horses and a pack animal, two months worth of supplies and nobody looking for him here until roundup time in three or four weeks.

Tom sat up. "Wes, you never did say why you come up here with an extra horse with a saddle."

"Didn't. Found the critter on the trail. Looked like he'd been run real hard for a time. Saw some buzzards congregating a couple of miles over. Figure it could have been the horse's owner. You hear about anybody riding the hootowl trail up in here who might have been wanted?"

"Nary a one. Just wondered. Not a lot of horses wandering around way up in here. No problem. We'll talk in the morning."

It took Wes a half hour to go to sleep. Tom dropped off almost at once and snored softly. Wes wondered if he was faking the sleep.

Wes at last dropped off but came awake some time later, the six-gun in his hand. It was still dark. A board in the shack floor creaked.

"Damn, didn't mean to wake you," Tom said. "Just got to water the old lily. Be right back."

Wes shivered as he let the hammer down silently on the hot round in his six-gun. He held the weapon until Tom slipped back into the shack and took to his blankets.

Wes wasn't sure if he'd sleep anymore that night. What if Tom wasn't who he said he was. Maybe he was one of the bank robbers. He'd

36

found the shack, identified his leader's horse and would keep Wes here until the rest of the gang arrived with lots of rifles and shotguns. Wes worried it. He was sure he would never get back to sleep.

He did, waking up a little after daylight. Tom came awake about the same time, and they both kicked out of blankets and pulled on pants and boots.

"Breakfast?" Wes asked.

Tom nodded. "Yeah, but I don't want you to run short on grub. I know you got just so much rations for so many days before you get resupplied. I ain't all dumb about ranching."

"Roundup crew will be this way in three or four weeks. I can spare another breakfast. I appreciate your thought."

Tom went out to look at his new mount and put his saddle blanket and saddle on the big roan. As soon as he was out the door, Wes dug under his bunk for the saddlebags. They were still there, and the two packets of bills were there. They were bundles of twenty-dollar notes. Wes had no idea how much money was in each stack. He pushed the stacks of notes inside his shirt and went back to working on a breakfast of hot cakes, syrup and sausages.

An hour later Tom stepped into his saddle.

"I like this animal. She's got a lot more depth than my old nag. This one won't have trouble with shins that splint."

"How far to your ranch?"

"I go through the breaks over west, and I should be there in a day and a half."

"You take care. Keep your eyes open. I heard something about a bank robbery before I left the ranch, but don't know where it was. Some owlhoots might be riding in this direction to get away from a posse."

Tom reached down and shook Wes's hand. "Thanks, friend. If we ever meet again, the beer and the biggest supper in the cafe are both on me."

They waved and Tom Swanson rode off to the west. Wes watched him until he was out of sight. Then he cleaned up the breakfast dishes. Outside he found the hasp and twenty-penny nail that locked the door to keep out skunks and any other creatures who wanted to share his food, then he checked the spring.

He cleaned it out, removing leaves and grass so it flowed pure. It dribbled from a crack in a rock and didn't look like it would produce much, but over twenty-four hours it brought a lot of water to the tiny seep that worked down to and into the thirsty ground for thirty yards.

He moved and the stack of bills inside his shirt scraped against his skin, and he thought about the money. He took out the two packets of bills and checked them. Yes, both bundles of twenty-dollar greenbacks.

He bent them up on the end and counted up to twenty. He had only started. He went right back to the shack and inside where he sat at the makeshift table and counted the two bundles of money. There were five hundred bills in each group. That was ten thousand dollars times two. Twenty thousand dollars. Where did the lone rider get twenty thousand dollars except from the Long Grass Territorial Bank?

What was he going to do about the twenty thousand dollars? Just as important, he knew that one man seldom robbed a bank. It took a whole gang of men. So where were the others, and what would they do when they found the gunsharp dead, his horse gone and the money missing?

Wes Parker knew at once what they would do. Question him and then torture him to tell them where he hid the money and in the end they would kill him.

Wes had learned one thing from Tom Swanson. "Oh damn!" Wes said and stuffed the money back in the bank bag. He had to find a good place to hide it but not in the line shack.

Three

Wes went outside and stared around the spring and shack searching for the ideal place to conceal the cash. The shack was the first place they would tear apart. On the small rise to the north, a scattering of small trees stood. A dozen scrub pine of some kind. Too obvious. Or was it? He walked the fifty yards up there and saw that the trees were larger than he thought.

He climbed one of the pines until he was twenty feet off the ground. There were lots of branches, and he had to work through them to get that high. Just above him, three branches came out from the same spot on the foot-thick trunk, forming a crotch. He reached up and placed the leather bag in the crotch. It balanced there nicely, and he decided it couldn't be seen from the ground.

From his pocket he took a three-foot strip of leather thong and tied the pouch securely in place. Then he climbed down and looked at the spot. Nothing could be seen of the bank bag.

He noted the tree carefully. It was the one closest to the line shack, that should be easy to remember.

Back at the shelter, Wes packed himself a lunch, a cheese sandwich, an apple and a canteen of fresh water. He took a notebook and two sharp pencils in his saddlebags and rode out to the north. Canada was just up that way a spell. He'd never been in Canada, hadn't even seen it.

He had ridden only a half mile when he found some Bar-N cattle, three cows and calves, six yearling steers and two more that looked about market-ready. Most Montana ranges took four years to feed out a marketable steer.

He made an entry in his notebook about the cattle and their location and moved on. Another hundred yards north he found a faint trail that wound to the left, west. He studied it. Not a game trail. Only big game in this area would be the pronghorn antelope. The trail showed only shod hooves, so it must be the one Old Jed had used as his northern boundary. Along that trail five miles was the spot where someone had shot Old Jed.

Was the same man waiting there? Was it his regular guard station? What was he protecting? Wes stared to the west for a while, wondering.

Then he turned west and rode. He found dozens more cattle, some above the trail and some below. He counted them by age and sex and put them down in his book.

He sat a moment on a little rise and stared

41

across the countryside. It was open, quiet, serene. No loud talk, just the gentle wind singing in the grass. To the left he thought he saw a flash of red, then it was gone. He sat there and stared north. As far as he could see there wasn't a fence post, not a house or barn, not a buggy or a locomotive. It was pure, unsullied wilderness, the open grasslands.

Wes sat his mount for ten minutes, watching the wind in the grass, spying a hawk with its jagged end wings and hook nose soaring higher and higher in an updraft of heated air. The sun was out warm but not yet hot. He sipped at his canteen of water, then rode on down the faint line rider's trail that Old Jed had left.

Wes came to the spot he considered five miles from the shack and he looked around. Yes, some brush, a few trees to the right, the start of a ridge and what looked like could be some breaks and a small valley or two to the far front.

Was this the place where Old Jed had been shot? He had no way of knowing. He paused and took out the Spencer and carried it across the saddle. Wouldn't hurt. After a long look at the brushy spot, he turned back to the trail and continued.

The farther west he went, the closer he came to some breaks he could see in the distance. They held more trees and might work as a future site for a better line shack. At least there would be more firewood around.

He stopped about noon when the sun was almost overhead and ate his sandwich and apple.

He checked his critter count and found more animals than he thought would be in this section. He had just touched the northern edge of the range. There was a huge area to the south the riders would sweep, driving the cattle north during the roundup. They would herd the cattle into various central locations in each sector to check them, brand the new ones and cut out all the steers ready for market.

He saw a wolf slinking into a patch of timber when he reached the far side of what he considered would be the end of his trail. To the left in the edge of the light timbered slopes, he saw the opening of a small valley. Curious, he rode into it and looked around. It was no more than a quarter of a mile long and about half that wide. It looked like a large corral. What a perfect spot to hold some cattle for roundup. He rode partway into the little valley to check the graze. It was still a foot high and a kind of grass that most of the cattle liked. He figured he was fourteen to fifteen miles from the line shack by that time.

He made a note to remember the place and was almost out of the valley when he noticed charcoal at one side. Someone had built a fire there, a good sized one from the chunks of half-burned wood they had left.

Much too large for cooking. He studied it a bit and saw a lot of boot prints in the dirt around the fire. Off to the side, he noticed a matted-down place where blanket rolls could have been spread. On a ways, he found another smaller fire and bits of wrappers and a can that had once contained sliced peaches and dirt that still smelled like bacon grease. Someone had used this valley. What for? Was the fire the key? At once the image of a ruthless band of rustlers came to mind.

Impossible. This was the middle of the Bar-N ranch. Well, not the middle, the upper slopes of the ranch, but totally controlled by the Bar-N. How could anyone get in here and rustle cattle? Even if they did, there was no reasonable route to get them out to the Montana market or rail line without crossing a lot of Bar-N land.

He shrugged and rode on out. It was a wild idea, but he wouldn't forget the valley entirely. Might come in handy to hold some cattle or even quarantine some from a bad disease.

The faint track he had been following west continued, so he kept riding forward. He came to a small stream running to the south. That was where the trail stopped. He found some evidence of a campfire and horse droppings where Old Jed evidently had left his mount overnight.

He had just turned around and began heading back the way he came when he flushed a pheasant out of the edge of the trail. The big bird had huddled down trying to avoid moving, but when the shod hooves hit the dirt too close to her, she rose up with a frantic beating of wings and gained about twenty feet, then glided as far as she could away from the intruder.

Intruder. Yes, he felt like an intruder in this pristine wonderland. It must be the way it was five hundred years ago. Nothing would have changed. Perhaps the course of a stream or river, the type of grasses, maybe trees had swept down farther on the high ridges.

As he stared at the landscape, he thought of the Indian wars, and how the Indians were being driven off their hunting grounds by the land-hungry settlers and ranchers. He sighed. They called it progress. Manifest Destiny. Right now he could see the Indians' side of it.

A meadowlark called from a low bush down the trail. He saw some kind of ground squirrels working around mounds of dirt and holes.

Wes checked the land with a critical eye. Old Jed had been right. There was no chance anyone would try to rustle stock to the north. Nothing up there but wilderness, Canadian wilderness and no market for American beef.

To the west, a series of breaks and small hills showed. Rough country that any cowboy would have fits trying to drive a herd of beef through. Rustlers would surely pick an easier spot. Someone stealing Bar-N beef from this area was way down on his list of worries. He kept a closer eye out on the return trip to check on sick or down cattle. He found none this time. But it was amazing how quickly a herd could develop black leg or lump jaw. He had the standard line rider's kit of medicines behind him on the saddle. He wouldn't be a veterinarian exactly, but he was expected to take care of the minor problems in the cattle before they developed so far they killed the animal.

On the way home, when he came to the five-mile point where Old Jed had been shot, he galloped into the screening brush and burst through it, but found nothing. No evidence that anyone had spent any time there. No charcoal, no trash, not even any horse droppings. He searched an area fifty yards across, found nothing and returned to the trail.

It was dusk by the time he rode up to the shack. He saw the spot of color again dart into the tall grass and then step out, boldly watching him. Wes identified the fully grown red fox. It had a left ear that drooped slightly. The fox tensed, watched him ride up to within thirty feet of him, then it ran away half that distance and stopped and turned.

This was the same red fox he had seen before. He knew now because he remembered the lop ear. The fox wasn't as frightened as most wild animals would be in this situation. For a moment, Wes wondered if Old Jed had made a pet of the fox. He shook his head. Not with Pochuck. Old Jed's dog looked part hound, and he wouldn't hold truck getting friendly with a red fox.

Wes rode on, put his horse near the spring so she could drink, then unsaddled her and hung the saddle on a post that had been planted in the ground probably for that purpose. He picketed Matilda where she could find some graze and still reach water and turned toward the shack.

The fox had returned. Now it sat with ears

pricked forward watching him. It was six feet from the shack door, waiting and watching.

Wes walked slowly toward the fox, the notebook in one hand against his leg, his other hand behind his back. When Wes came within ten feet of the fox, it turned and trotted away that far and sat down and watched him again.

Wes wondered if his voice would frighten the wild creature. He began talking softly, low and with concern.

"Well, a small friend. Hello, red fox. Good to see you out here. Did Old Jed feed you?"

Again as Wes came within ten feet of the red fox, it pranced away, maintaining its distance.

When Wes reached the shack door, he pulled the twenty-penny nail out of the hasp, and let it hang by its string. He opened the door, and the fox ran off into the quickly falling darkness.

Inside, Wes lit a coal oil lamp and worked on his supper. He was hungry as a coyote on the prairie.

The next day Wes stayed at the shack. He cut wood at the small grove of trees up the slope. He found enough down and deadwood to last him the rest of the season. An axe and a six-foot crosscut saw were part of the shack's equipment, and he used them to good advantage. When he had enough wood cut and split, he put the pannier on the packhorse and led her up the slope where he filled the pack frame and tied on the wood.

He made three trips and had a generous stack

of cut and split firewood outside the shack door. He didn't see the red fox all that day.

The third day of his stay at Line Shack Twelve, he packed a larger lunch, put it in the saddlebags, took his canteen and his Spencer rifle and notebook and worked the eastern section of his domain.

Again he came on a game trail that had been made mostly by Old Jed. Here he found some prints of the elusive antelope. He sat on his horse and scanned the long sweep of land around him but could see only an occasional splotch of grazing cattle. Nowhere did he spot any of the pronghorn antelope. If he could find one in range of his Spencer, he'd bring it down if he could. He could eat on fresh meat for two days, maybe three before it went rancid.

If he did get an antelope, he'd try to sun dry thin strips of meat into jerky. The Indians did it. Why couldn't he? As he remembered, it would take three days on drying pegs in the sun for the thin-sliced meat to dry so it would keep without spoiling. He could do that.

This side of the spread looked more like the great plains, with the land slanting off in unending waves of grass, small rises and gentle inclines but with the horizon a straight line for a hundred and eighty degrees. There were no breaks or hills on this side, no majestic mountains in the distance, just the fine grass and good graze for the Bar-N cattle.

He checked the animals and found one that could be developing black leg. He made a spe-

48

cial note of the area, about how far from the shack and the only geographic landmark, a small, raw dirt cliff twenty feet high that rose up from the plains for no reason he could determine.

The brood cow was only starting to develop some of the characteristics of black leg, but it would do no harm to treat her now. He rode up beside her, gentled her down and then bullied her into standing still for a few seconds so he could smear the thick brown salve on her right fore leg from hoof to knee. She gave him only those few seconds, then shook her horns at him, and he backed away as she snorted and galloped fifty feet across the grass before she slowed and stopped and went back to grazing.

Wes grinned at the bovine, mounted Matilda and worked through the herd making notes on his pad, detailing the cows and calves, steers, yearlings and range bulls.

The sweep around this side of the trail left by the many trips by Old Jed proved to be easier, quicker and less productive. The distances were hard to reckon with the horizon edging farther and farther away with each mile traveled toward it. The flowing grass and spots of cattle seemed to go on forever.

About two in the afternoon, the trail he followed came to an abrupt halt at a small dry streambed. Evidently it was some kind of a marker for Old Jed, and Wes turned Matilda around and worked back along the fifteen-mile route he had covered.

He saw one steer he figured had lump jaw, but by the time he got near the critter, it took off like a just-branded maverick and he never did catch up to it. He marked the malady in his notebook and the approximate location. Next time he'd be sure to have a bottle of Fleming's Lump Jaw Cure with him to treat the beast.

The rest of the ride home went peacefully. He enjoyed the wide open country. The sky looked a mile high here, bright blue and without the trace of a cloud. From horizon to horizon he could see nothing but the still green Montana grass speckled with brown and black of the Bar-N range cattle. He felt strangely at ease, pleased that he decided to take this line rider's job. For a few moments he forgot all about the gunman on the trail and who it was who had shot Old Jed.

Back at the line shack, he watered Matilda, then put a saddle on the packhorse and rode her around the shack and up to the woods on the slope. She needed some exercise so she didn't wither away to nothing. The mare seemed to enjoy the work, and when she came back, she drank well at the spring and then munched contentedly on the grass.

He fried the last of the bacon to start his supper, then boiled some cut up carrots and boiled a few potatoes. He tried to make bacon gravy, but it turned out to be mostly lumpy flour, water and bacon grease, but all in all it worked out to a fairly good meal. Filling at least, and he had half of the food left over for tomorrow.

He was stoking the fire when the shack door jerked open and the double barrels of a shotgun poked through the opening. Wes had no time to dive for his six-gun he had left belted and hung on the chair.

Behind the shotgun came the dirtiest man Wes had ever seen. The only word Wes could think of was "rawhider," and it sent a series of deadly chills down his spine. Rawhiders, men and women with no morals whatsoever, who steal and kill and take what they want and burn and destroy the rest. He'd heard of such men but never met one.

The man behind the sawed-off scatter gun had matted brown hair, a scraggly beard inter-rupted by pimples, and sores that erupted from the beard and covered the rest of his face in a pitted wasteland. His forehead held an open wound, probably from a knife slash. It had started to heal around the edges, but the three-inch length gaped open a quarter of an inch at the center.

"Food!" the man gasped. He saw the leftover food on the rough table and stumbled toward it, grabbing a handful of the boiled potatoes and pushing it into his mouth. The barrels of the big gun never wavered from Wes's belly.

The man wore a shirt with one button. His skin through the top of the shirt was sunburned and black from caked dirt. The arms of the shirt had been torn or cut off in ragged tatters, and his forearms were masses of sores and grime.

His fingernails had been broken off until there was little left of them beyond the quick.

He stuffed the carrots in his mouth and bellowed something toward the door before he finished chewing.

Another tattered semblance of a man came through the opening. He could barely walk. He hobbled on a crutch made from the limb of a tree. His eyes were so deep set, his face looked like a skull. His clothes were shabbier and dirtier than the first man's.

He lunged for the table, knocked the other man down, and the shotgun went off, blasting a load of buckshot into the ceiling. The first rawhider quickly righted himself and pointed the scatter gun back at Wes.

"See what woulda happened to you, young guy, if you'd been in front of that? Wham!"

They ate the rest of the food on the table, and the last one who came in drew a ten-inch fighting knife from his much-patched and torn-apart pants.

"Food!" he demanded in a voice barely human.

"I'll have to cook something," Wes said.

"Do it. Whiskey. You got any whiskey?"

Wes shook his head. He hadn't even considered bringing any with him. He didn't drink much. No cause to out here.

"Then cook food!" the rawhider shouted.

Wes used his knife and cut a big "X" in a tin of canned peaches. He dumped them into two bowls and put a metal spoon with each one. The fruit vanished down their throats almost as soon as he set the dishes down.

"More!" the man with the knife bawled.

Wes knew his only hope to stay alive was to do what they said. They both were in poor shape. He had to wait until they slept, then he could get their weapons and in the morning he'd send them on their way. He hadn't heard any horses. His animals hadn't done any horse talk. Maybe the two were on foot.

The only thing they could be doing way up here was running. A posse must be on their tail. When he was of no use to them, they would kill him without a thought. He knew that. He had to strike before they gained enough strength to overpower him.

Wes cooked potatoes, sliced off two big chunks of ham and put them in a skillet and let them brown, then heated them through by letting them boil in the pan.

By the time the potatoes were cooked, the ham slices had been eaten and forgotten. He poured a dozen cut-up potatoes into bowls, and the men burned their fingers picking them up and munching them down without benefit of utensils or manners.

"That's enough," Wes told them. "You eat any more, and you'll just throw it up and be worse off than before. You both need rest. Lay down on the bunk and get some sleep. In the morning I'll have bacon and flapjacks for you, all you can eat."

The second man who had come inside had

fallen asleep at the table. The taller one slapped him awake, pointed to the bunk, and he stumbled to the bed and rolled on it asleep as soon as he stretched out.

The shotgun man lifted Wes's .45 from the holster hanging on the chair and waved it at Wes. "Don't want you thinking about hurting us when we go to sleep. Gonna have to tie you up. You're a good cook so we need you till we feel better. Damn near starved to death out there in that damn desert of grass."

He leaned to one side and took a quick step so he wouldn't fall down. "Don't go and try to be no hero. We'll just feed ourselves a couple of days and ride out on them two horses of yours. Ours got themselves shot up and died a ways back."

The rawhider put the shotgun on the table and rubbed one hand over his face. "Been a damn long day. Sit yourself down at the chair there whilest I tie you up. You kin sleep sitting up jist fine."

Furiously Wes tried to think of something. If he objected, he might be killed as a matter of convenience. He slumped in the chair so he would have room to work on the knots. He'd brought in a spare lariat to work on, and the rawhider picked it up and made a loop and settled it around Wes's waist, pinning his hands at his sides.

"Yep, should work." He made two more loops with the rope around the chair and then stood in front of Wes for a moment. He let down the six-gun to tie a knot with both hands.

From where he sat, Wes kicked upward with

his foot as hard as he could. His heavy boot hit the rawhider's inner thigh, skidded upward and slammed hard into the man's scrotum, smashing his testicles high against his pelvic bones and crushing one of the orbs.

The killer started to screech in pain just as Wes kicked him again in the same place. The man dropped the rope, held his crotch with both hands and slumped to the floor unconscious from the pain.

Wes pushed with his hands, jiggled the chair, got the rope to swing around. He worked it again and pulled his hands against the strands, soon loosening them enough to lift his arms upward and get his hands free. He pulled the rope off himself and used it to tie the injured man moaning on the floor. Wes bound his ankles together, then with the same rope looped it up and tied his wrists tightly to one another.

He found some rawhide thongs on a shelf and gently laced the sleeping man's feet together. Then he rolled the man over without waking him up and tied his hands behind him.

Wes gave a little sigh of relief as he finished the knots. Maybe he wouldn't die here on the high lonely after all.

He had these two well in hand. Had they brought horses or not? He pushed open the door and looked outside. In the shadows of the moonlight he saw another man sitting against the woodpile, aiming a sawed-off shotgun squarely at his chest.

Four

Wes stared through the dim light of a new moon at the shotgunner. "Easy, take it easy," Wes said. "I'm supposed to tell you it's your time to come inside."

Wes said it in the most soothing tones he could muster. The shock of seeing another shotgun pointed at him was almost too much. The man didn't reply.

"Hey, no problem, what do you want me to do?" Wes said.

Still the man said nothing. Was he sleeping?

"I'll come over there, and we can talk better." The woodpile was against the front of the shack, less than ten feet from the doorway. Wes took two steps forward, then two more. The shotgunner didn't move. Then in a rush Wes ran forward and lunged at the man, toppling him over where he sat. He hit the ground like a dead weight, and the shotgun fell from his fingers but didn't go off.

Strange. Wes stood and picked up the shotgun

and kicked the man's legs gently. He didn't respond. Wes rolled him over on his back. His knees stayed bent. Then Wes saw the blood on the man's shirt and throat. His lifeless eyes gazed back at him. The man had been dead for some time.

Wes left him and made a quick circuit around the shack. He found one horse with blood on the saddle about thirty yards from the shelter. Three men. All rawhiders who must have been in a gun fight.

The one man said their horses had been shot up and died. Who fought back against the rawhiders? There wasn't a ranch within thirty miles or more. Maybe a posse was chasing them. He walked the horse to the spring and let it drink. It had blood on it but didn't seem to be wounded. He tied it to a bit of brush near his other two mounts.

What should he do with the pair of rawhiders? He had no proof they were law violators. He couldn't let them starve. On the other hand, in a few days they'd eat him out of half of his supplies.

One fact was certain. He'd have to bury the dead one. Maybe he could get some information out of the other two. He went back into the shack. Both men were still sleeping. He searched them, found each had a hideout derringer, and he took them. He got knives from each as well and decided they were free of weapons. He found no identification of any kind on either man.

They smelled so bad he hated to be near them. He'd done his time without a bath on a trail drive, but he smelled sweet compared to these two. Must have been a year since either of them had even fallen in a creek.

By that time it was after nine o'clock. He turned the coal-oil lamp down low and took a pair of blankets outside. Wes made himself a soft pad and lay down staring at the sky full of stars. He'd figure out what to do with this pair in the morning.

He awoke about four-thirty. Only a few streaks of light in the dark east. He heard a scream from the shack. One before this must have been what awakened him. He went to the shack and looked in the door. The rawhider he'd left on the floor was awake and killing mad.

"What the hell? What's going on? Who the hell tied me up?"

Wes nudged the rawhider's leg with his boot. "I tied you up. You go back to sleep. You've got a lot of questions to answer in the morning."

"Bastard!" the man screeched.

"Shut up or I'll put a gag on you. You want that?"

The man glared at Wes, who turned and went outside to his blankets. They weren't so soft this time, and he didn't get back to sleep before the stabbing rays of sunlight suddenly burst over the prairie. It went from dark to light in only a few seconds.

He sat up and rubbed the sleep from his eyes, went to the spring and had a long drink, then checked inside the shack. Both the rawhiders were awake and swearing at him. The food they ate last night had given them more energy this morning, and they spewed their rage on Wes.

He yelled at them to be quiet. Neither one calmed down. Wes took a dipper of cold water and threw it in the face of each rawhider. That shocked them into shutting up.

"Now, I'm asking the questions, and if you want anything to eat ever again in your dirty lives, you better answer me straight. Understand?" One man nodded. The other glared.

"Is a posse chasing you?"

"Was, we ditched them, stupid bastards."

"Why was the posse after you?"

"They don't like us," one rawhider said.

"Yeah, they think we're a bad influence on their little town."

"What did you do in the town? Was it Long Grass?"

"Yeah, so what?"

"Did you kill somebody?"

Both men laughed. Wes gave up and went for a fresh bucket of water. He'd heard enough. If a posse from Long Grass was after them, he could take them back to the ranch, and they'd send word to the posse. Take them when? Today? They probably weren't strong enough to sit a horse. At least he had three mounts so they wouldn't have to ride double.

He'd feed them today, get them stronger and take them to the ranch tomorrow morning. That decided, he carried the bucket of fresh water back to the shack. He hesitated before he went in. He heard them talking.

". . . I don't see how the hell we're gonna do that," one of the men said.

"Easy. I get a kitchen knife to cut up some food, then when he comes close, I stab the shithead in the chest. Then we can stay here for a week or two. Leave when we want to."

"Maybe find another little ranch like that one outside of town?" the other voice asked. "Jeez, but that blond woman was good. Three times I did her. She got to like it there at the end. I got her two times, then she tried to stab me, so I choked her while I was still humping her. Damn, that was wild."

Wes stepped into the shack. "Did you kill all of them at the ranch?"

The younger of the two on the floor snorted. "What the fuck if we did? None of your business. When do we get something to eat?"

"You don't. Now shut up while I get myself some breakfast. Then the three of us are going for a long ride." Wes had changed his plans. He better get to the ranch today.

"What the hell, I can't even sit a horse," the one with the black beard on the floor wailed.

"Tough. I'll tie you belly-down over the saddle. I don't much care if you get to the ranch dead or alive."

Wes had breakfast as the two rawhiders brayed and bellowed, demanding food. He ignored them. Next he dug a shallow grave for the third rawhider. He found a letter on the body and kept it. He filled in the three-foot deep hole after rolling the body into it. All he needed was enough dirt to keep the animals from smelling the corpse.

By eight o'clock he had the three horses saddled and at the shack. He brought out the younger one from the floor. Cut his ankle ties but not those on his hands.

"You can do this easy on yourself or hard," Wes said. "I don't give a damn. No, wrong. Fact is I'd love to smash you up a bit, so don't give me a reason. You want to sit in the saddle or belly over it?"

"Sit," the man said. Most of his bravado was gone now. Wes helped him into the saddle. He'd tied the reins of the horse to the wall so she couldn't be ridden off. Wes bound the rawhider's hands to the saddle horn.

"You fall off or try to get off, you'll be dragged for a while. So use your head and sit still."

He brought out the other man who was worse off physically. He had a gunshot wound in his leg and another one high up in his chest that must have missed his lung.

Wes gave him the same lecture. He chose to sit the saddle. Wes tied the two horses on lead ropes one behind the other, then put the nail through the hasp on the door and headed for the ranch.

Tom Swanson's cow pony had recovered from her leg bruise and moved out well. The pack-horse, used to more weight than was on her back, stepped along like a young colt. Wes set a fast pace, walking the horses at five miles an hour when the terrain permitted, which was most of the time.

He knew the route now, and cut off a pair of wide arcs he had made before. By noon he figured they had made a little over fifteen miles. He untied one hand for the rawhiders, but tied their feet as he let them get off their mounts for a quick noon meal.

He had made ham sandwiches before they left, using up the last of the pork. He watched them with his six-gun in hand as they ate. Wes knew they were waiting for him to make that one mistake so they could try to escape.

He didn't make any mistakes. He put one rawhider at a time back on his mount, tied his feet together under the horse's belly, then tied both hands to the saddle horn again.

"You bastard!" the younger one screamed. "Know what I'm gonna do to you when I get loose? Gonna skin you like a veal. Pull your skin off before I kill you and watch you squirm and scream and bellow in agony."

Wes snorted. "Give me an excuse, rawhider. Just give me one excuse, and I'll put four rounds right through your heart and belly you down for the rest of the ride. You want that?"

The rawhider quieted and the ride continued. They were over the last low ridge and within sight of the ranch buildings about five miles out, when the younger rawhider made his break.

He had pulled the lead rope back and chewed

it in two with his teeth. Wes felt a different tension on the lead lines behind and turned just as the rawhider kicked the packhorse in the flanks and jerked her head to the left and she galloped away. Wes turned and raced after him. He still had the second horse on a lead behind him. He cut it loose, and galloped toward the big packhorse.

It took Wes a quarter of a mile to catch the other mount. He grabbed the reins and pulled the horse to a stop. Then he drew his six-gun and slammed it down across the rawhider's forehead. The killer slumped to the side and screeched in fury and pain. Two long blood lines showed on his forehead and one down his cheek. He kept his saddle because he was still tied on.

"Try that again and you're as dead as your friend I buried back at the cabin. I won't warn you again."

Wes led the horse back to where the Slash S animal waited. The other rider had been half out of his mind on the ride. Evidently he didn't realize his mount was free. Wes tied the lead ropes on again and watched both men as he trailed them on into the ranch.

He met two cowboys about a mile out.

"What the hell you got there, Wes?" one asked.

"A pair of murdering rawhiders. I figure we can cut them up and feed them to the hogs."

"Damn, you catch them both?"

Wes laughed. "No, they rode in and gave themselves up."

At the ranch, Caleb met Wes at the corral.

"Damn, Wes, looks like you turned into a lawman. Sheriff was past just yesterday warning us about these gents. Said there was three of them."

"Was. One died on the woodpile. I got a letter off him. He's Charlie Snyder. Or he was. He'd been shot up pretty bad."

"We won't feed them too much," Caleb said. "Bread and water sounds about right. These are the ones who hit a little ranch below Long Grass. Raped and killed two women, killed four hands and the owner, then burned down all the buildings and stole everything they thought they could sell. Sheriff said they had a covered wagon jammed full of stolen goods. They killed two in the posse before they got away. Sheriff'll be damn glad to get them.

"I'll send a man into town so he can come out. Boys, lock these two in the feed shed, that end room. I want a guard on them until the sheriff gets here."

"How is Old Jed?" Wes asked.

"Feeling better. The doc came and dug out the slug. Said it should have killed him. He'll be up and around in a few more days, but he won't be doing any more riding work. I'll find something for him around the home place here. Told him he would die on this ranch, but not for a lot of years yet."

They walked toward the kitchen.

"Oh, the sheriff said there was a reward for these no-goods. Five hundred dollars. I'll tell him it's yours."

Wes nodded. "I heard about rewards before that never happened. If it does, put it in the bank for me."

"Sure will. Hope it don't get robbed. Sheriff said he's been watching for four bank robbers, too. They hit the bank in Long Grass and headed north. They split up, and three of them got away from a posse. They got the one with the slowest horse. Shot him out of the saddle."

"Appears we're having a crime wave out here," Wes said. He hadn't decided yet what to do with the money. There were still two of the gang, and they'd be hunting the man who had all the loot. They might come his way, and they might not.

"Oh, I rode out there where Old Jed said he got shot. Couldn't find anything, no hoof marks, no trash, no place where somebody had been standing guard."

"Wasn't Old Jed's imagination," Caleb said. "That .45 caliber lead slug proves that. Just watch yourself up there. You have supper with us, stay the night, and the cook will send you some more good eating stuff when you hightail it out of here in the morning."

After supper, Wes talked with Old Jed in his room. The old man sat in a chair, grinning, his leg up on a pillow.

"Hell, boy, I ain't had it so good since I got married for the first time back in eighteen and thirty-eight. You wasn't even born by then. I'm eating high off the shoat, get waited on, got no work to do and still drawing my pay!"

Wes grinned. "Which must mean you're getting sick of sitting around this way. You could at least make some long splices in the end of the working rider's lariats so they work smooth."

They laughed. Wes poured Old Jed another cup of coffee.

"You ever see a red fox up at the shack?" Wes asked.

"You mean Frisky? Yeah. Used to feed him now and then. He's a big male, and I figure he's got a couple of lady friends nearby, but I never saw them. He got right friendly for a while."

"I've seen him a couple of times. Gonna take some work for him to get used to me, I'd guess. What does he like to eat?"

"Almost anything. He ain't fussy." Old Jed paused. "You ain't seen that gunman up there, have you?"

Wes told him he tried to find the ambush spot but couldn't.

"Gol dang! Wish I knowed who he was. Raked over my brain cells a dozen times, and I can't fancy what anybody would be doing up there. Now that I figure on it, don't think he was trying to hit me with them shots, just scare me off."

Wes didn't ask about the little valley he'd found. He talked about other things, and then said goodbye and turned in at the bunkhouse on an empty cot. He was glad Old Jed was feeling better. Wes passed up the poker game going on at the front of the bunkhouse. He wanted to get to sleep now so he could get an early start in the morning.

The next day, the ride back to Line Shack Twelve was routine. He looked for the remains of the bank robber, but even though he thought he had the same route, he could be a mile or two one way or the other and never know it in these grasslands. He didn't spot any buzzards, so the big birds must have finished their work and looked for another feast.

He set off early from the Bar-N and made it back to the line shack just before dark. He felt as if he'd been in the saddle for a year and a half. No one cooked in the shack as he came up to it. No one poked a shotgun in the door. Just as well. He was as tired as a newborn calf on a roundup.

He scrambled eggs the cook at the ranch had packed for him. The cook had broken the eggs and put eight of them in a pint fruit jar and sealed the top. Wes had half of them for supper and saved the others for breakfast. Next time he went back to the ranch he should bring up six laying hens and a milk cow. Wes chuckled and shook his head. Not a chance.

Morning brought a bright sun with some thunderheads coming in from the west, but they probably wouldn't drop any rain. A mild thunderstorm or two was not unusual in the summer, but it just didn't feel right to Wes.

He had breakfast and mounted Matilda for a leisurely ride around the west sector. He took a gunny sack on the back of his saddle filled with every cow medication he had. He'd be ready this time.

He moved along slowly, noting the animals, counting them again, comparing. Not much difference between now and a few days ago. He made his entries in his log as usual and passed right through the five-mile point where Old Jed figured he got shot at. Nothing happened again, and Wes began to think the old man might have the wrong spot.

He found a black leg cow and treated her with the salve, then helped a newborn get his legs. Its larger size indicated it was a late born calf. Wes sat on the ground watching the hour-old calf trying to get to his feet. On the third try he made it and wobbled over to his mother and tried to nurse. He fell down.

Wes grinned. In another hour he would be nursing and running around enough to worry his mother.

Wes had fixed roast beef sandwiches for his lunch. The cook sent along two big slabs of roast, warning him to eat it up by the end of the second day so he didn't get sick.

He worked the west side of the range to the end of the trail and paused, looking around. Nothing that shouldn't be there. No dust clouds of riders, no smoke. He turned and worked the route back the other way, finding a few more cattle he hadn't seen when coming up.

Back at the shack, he watered Matilda and picketed her in a grassy spot where she could still reach the water.

For supper, he had the rest of the roast with some pure ground horseradish that made him sputter and grab for his coffee to temper the blowing-the-top-of-his-head-off sensation. His eyes watered, and he vowed to thin out the horseradish with some water before he had another bite.

He put some beans to soak. He still had the ham bone he'd use to flavor them. He'd heard it took two days of soaking and then about four hours to cook the hard dried beans. He'd find out for sure as he did it.

Twice the next day he felt as if someone was watching him. Nothing he could point to. No flash of a field glass in the sunlight. No call from a far-off horse smelling Matilda. He'd left the packhorse at the ranch so she'd be rested for the next trip out. That wouldn't come until after roundup. Now it looked like it was still three more weeks away before they would get near Shack Twelve.

He cut a little more wood, split some of the dead pine into fine kindling and put it in a rack in front of the stove wood. He used a shovel and dug out a bigger pond below the spring. If it got hot enough, he could strip down and sit in the water and cool off. He worked a little on expanding the pool the next three days and couldn't shake the idea someone was watching every move he made.

The problem of the twenty thousand dollars was never far from his thoughts. From what Caleb said at the ranch, there were still two of the gang on the loose. Had they taken to the trail and put as many miles between them and the gone-wrong robbery as they could? Or were they still looking for Liberty, who Wes figured must have been their leader and carried all the money until they split it up.

Half a dozen times he wanted to go up the slope to the pine woods and check the tree to be sure the leather bank bag was still where he had tied it. It had to still be there. Any such move on his part would be a dead giveaway where the loot was if someone was watching him.

He put a hasp inside the door on the shack and pushed a twenty-penny nail through it at night now. He'd be less apt to be caught empty-handed that way if somebody tried to break in at night.

Every day now Wes saw the red fox; Frisky, Old Jed had called him. Wes tried using the name and the fox turned, cocked his head and started at Wes. For the first time, Wes tried to feed the fox. He had some old T-bones from steaks the cook had given him.

Wes held one out and Frisky caught the scent, but he would come no closer than ten feet. Even there his ears were pricked, his nose quivering and his tail swishing slowly in anticipation of a hasty retreat.

Wes left the bone and walked away from it.

Frisky approached it cautiously, sniffed it, then grabbed it and scurried away twenty feet, sat down and began chewing on the tough bovine bone.

Wes watched the fox for a half hour that night. Frisky stayed after he worked over the bone. He was still there when Wes walked into the shack and lit a lamp.

Wes heard a soft yapping from outside, then all was quiet except for a big horned owl who had taken a claim on one of the pine trees up the slope. Wes hoped the owl didn't find the leather bag and use the twenty-dollar bills to build his nest.

The money made him think about the two gang members. Where were they? He looked at the pearl-handled Colt that he had taken off Liberty's body. It had been pushed to the back of the table. Might not be a good idea to leave it out in plain sight. Someone could recognize the distinctive revolver as Liberty's. Wes found a loose board in the floor of the shack and pried it up with his six-inch hunting knife. He wrapped the weapon in cloth, then a heavy piece of canvas and pushed it in the hole under the floorboard. He placed the floorboard back in place and stomped on it to make sure it was set, then sat down on his bunk bed built against the wall.

He'd been cutting the tall grass around the spring and down on the slope. When it dried he'd stuff it into two gunny sacks he had and pin them together. Two of them would be enough for a makeshift mattress, but he wanted something better. Next time down to the ranch, he'd get some mattress ticking for a real sleeping pad. Yeah, that would be better. Until then, he'd try the gunny sacks with two blankets over them.

He stretched out on the hard boards for tonight and drifted off to sleep.

Morning came before he was ready. Wes scrambled out of his blankets, kicked into his boots and went out the door toward the two-foot hole he had dug as his open outhouse. He sensed something different. His frown deepened as he looked around his domain. Then his glance shot back to the spring. Matilda wasn't where he had staked her out last night.

Five

Wes looked around for his horse. She wasn't the kind to pull her picket and wander off. Evidently she had. Maybe something scared her. A mountain lion? Not way out here. Where could she be? All at once he realized that he didn't have his six-gun or rifle. He looked around casually, then started back into the shack. Wes was eight feet away and knew he'd never make it.

A rifle shot came with his second step and plowed up dirt six inches from his foot.

"Don't move again or you're one dead line rider," a voice called. It came from up the slope in the brush near the pine trees.

"We got three rifles on you, boy. You take one more step, and you'll be singing with the angels. Down on your knees, now!"

The voice came strong and clear. Nothing to do but what the man said. He went down to his knees and stared up the slope. Two men rode out of the brush, both with rifles aimed at him.

Wes snorted. They made their big mistake. They couldn't hit beans from horseback at fifty yards.

Wes dove to the side, rolled and scrambled to the door and lunged inside. Two shots scratched the ground around him on his move, but they missed. He grabbed his Spencer near the door and leaned out and sent a round at the two riders. They promptly turned and headed back to the brushy cover.

Wes didn't shoot again. He waited. He found the other five tubes of rounds for the Spencer and watched out the door from ground level. They wouldn't burn him out or try to shoot him out. They needed him or they wouldn't be here. Were they just looking for information, or did they know more than he hoped they did?

How? A slow chill settled on his backbone. Tom Swanson. They could have run into him before he got back to the Slash S. Could have. He tried to remember the horses they rode, but he didn't get a good enough look at them. If they spotted Tom, they'd recognize the big roan with the white blaze their leader had been astride. From then they would have questioned Tom until he told them where he got the animal. Then they came here.

He shivered. Tom Swanson probably didn't live through their torture. He'd hold out until they started cutting him. Then no man can keep quiet for long.

Wes sent two rounds into the brush out of frustration. No shots came in return. He fired the rest of his tube into the cover and figured he'd driven them back deeper into the trees. He took out the empty tube and pushed a full one into the Spencer, eased a loose round into the chamber and had eight rounds ready.

What now? They knew he was a line rider, so they would also realize they couldn't starve him out. If they needed him, they couldn't very well lay down a barrage of rifle fire and try to force him out. That way they could kill him.

He grinned, thinking that the two bank robbers must be hiding within a few dozen feet of the money they had come to find. Just then a bullet crashed through the top window pane in the front of the shack. Wes grinned. They were getting pissed because they had lost their advantage. They should have kept one gun on the ground and sent one rider down.

Morning. Damn long time to dark. After dark he could creep out, find their camp and shoot them or capture them. But what if they slipped into the shack while he was gone? Then they'd have the food and the advantage. He might have to risk it. He figured they'd try to parley long before then.

He sent another round into the brush and waited. It was the only hiding spot within half a mile of the shack. They didn't have many choices.

An hour later a call came from the brush.

"Hold your damn fire. You think this is a war or something?"

"You shot first, you bastard owlhoots. I don't take kindly to getting bushwhacked."

"We just want to talk."

"Strange way of talking, with your rifles."

"It's a tough country. Can't take chances."

"So talk."

Wes was still on the floor of the shack with the Spencer close to the door but not pushed out. He waited.

"Looking for a friend of ours. Maybe he stopped by here. Tall gent. Rode a big roan with a white blaze on her forehead. Strong mount. Said he was coming up this way."

"Why would he do that? This is cattle country, nothing else up here."

"He had a disagreement with the sheriff. Nothing major, just thought he'd ride the high country for a time. You seen him?"

"What's it worth to you if I did?"

"We don't got no cash money. Consider it a favor."

"Like the way you held me under two rifles? I ain't about to give you gents no favors. Rather give you some .52 caliber lead lunches."

There was a silence.

"Okay, so we made a mistake. We're a long way from town, and we're nervous up in this wild country. I'll be square with you. Our friend stole some money, and we're bound to find him and take him back to the sheriff."

Wes laughed. "You're a miserable liar. Your friend might have stole some money, and if he did, you probably helped him and he ran out with all the loot. You rob a store or a stage-coach?"

"We didn't rob nobody. He did. We want him. He's worth five thousand dollars reward. Dead or alive. So we're bounty hunters. Nothing wrong with that."

"Not until you start shooting at people. I seen your kind before. You get on your mounts and ride out of here, or I'm coming up there and blast you both into brimstone hell."

Wes thought of Liberty's letter and personal goods. Yes, he'd put that all in the bank bag with the money, so there was nothing in the shack to find except the six-gun.

Another silence stretched out.

The same voice came ten minutes later. "Cowboy, we got your sorrel up here. Damn pretty horse. Make you a bargain. You tell us what you know about our friend, and we won't shoot the horse. You keep talking the way you been, you're one line rider with a dead horse on his hands."

Wes scowled. They had the upper hand again. "You touch that animal and I'll scalp you alive, you hear me?"

"Hear you, don't think you could catch us on foot and us at a fancy trot across the grass. Think about it."

Wes beat his fist on the floor. He had to bend a little.

"Your friend have a name?"

"Yeah. Liberty. You seen him?"

Wes had them for sure then. Liberty was the name of the gent he'd killed back on the trail. "Nobody stopped by here with that name. Only

77

ones past here was a trio of rawhiders. I buried one, turned the other two over to the sheriff."

"You see Liberty on the trail? He was a tall gent, handled a six-gun real well."

"I don't get on the trail much. Work my line ride. That's about it. Now why don't you move on, hunt your friend where you might find him. He sure as hell ain't here."

Three rifle rounds slammed into the shack, one crashing through another foot square pane of glass in the front window.

The voice that came next was a different one. Older, rougher, with a bite to the words.

"Okay, little sombitch, we're through playing games with you. We know you saw Liberty. You had his horse. You gave it to some snot-nosed kid, and we took it away from him. We know you had the horse, and we know Liberty wouldn't give up his horse unless he's dead. So where the hell is the bank bag with the money?"

Wes put three more shots into the brush and heard a wail of protest. When the sound of the rifle fire echoed away across the grasslands, Wes yelled at the two men.

"What did you do to Tom Swanson?"

"The snot-nosed kid didn't want to answer our questions, so we persuaded him. Same fucking way we're gonna persuade you, bastard line rider. First we burn you out, then we cut you until you tell us where the money is. You got it, we want it."

Wes fired the rest of the tube of rounds into

78

the brush and hastily reloaded with a fresh tube and an eighth round in the chamber.

Nothing happened for five minutes. Then he saw a horse leave the brush. It was his mount, Matilda. A man rode her, leaning off to the side, giving almost no target. He carried a torch that Wes could see smoking. It was the Indian trick of riding off the horse to the side. But this white man had his foot hooked under the stirrup leather high up on the right side, and his leg slanted across Matilda's back. Wes thought of shooting the man in the leg, but the rifle round would slash through his leg and into Matilda. Not a chance he would do that. Wes could see a small slice of the robber's shoulder above the animal's back, but it was not a good target.

Matilda walked down the slope toward the shack. Twice Wes sighted in on a shoulder showing over Matilda's back, but each time he eased off. If he missed he could kill his favorite horse. The pair came closer. Wes figured about where the bank robber would lift up and throw the torch at the shack. It wouldn't do any good to throw it on the sod roof. He'd try for the window or the door and from no more than twenty feet.

Wes sighted in across the top of the sorrel, tracking the animal as it was ridden slowly downward. At thirty feet Matilda hesitated, then came on. The rider had her at a slight angle to the shack.

Wes slashed sweat off his forehead and

sighted in again just over Matilda's back. It was action-reaction time now. Like a fast draw.

It happened so suddenly that Wes was almost hypnotized into no action. The man heaved up, his left arm came out and up as he threw the blazing torch.

Just before the missile left the robber's hand, Wes lifted his sights and fired at the plainly showing chest. The bullet slammed out of the barrel and bored into the robber, jolting him backwards, his leg caught in the right stirrup leather over the back of Matilda.

The torch hadn't been thrown with full effort, and it fell to the ground six feet in front of the door and flamed briefly, then went out and smoked with the vapors drifting off to the east.

The robber on Matilda didn't make a sound. Wes saw the man's body sag off the horse to the far side and hang, head and arms down, with his right foot still trapped by the top of the stirrup leather and fender. Matilda stopped.

Four shots drilled into the edge of the shack door, splintering wood and forcing Wes to duck back to avoid the flying wood. He looked out the door again. The robber on Matilda still hung there, dead, Wes figured. He pushed the Spencer out the door and blasted four rounds into the brush, then two more. He replaced the tube in the weapon and angled it out the door.

He heard no more firing from the pine trees.

Wes called to Matilda. Usually she would come to him. Now she turned toward him, her eyes moving rapidly. The strange weight hanging down her side had her nearly in a state of panic.

Wes talked to her soothingly, calmed her down as best he could. But she wouldn't move another step.

Every five minutes for half an hour, Wes put three or four rounds into the woods near the pine trees. There was no response. He reloaded three empty tubes of ammunition for the Spencer, put a new tube in the stock and decided it was time to rush the hill. He could do it easier on Matilda.

He surged from the door to Matilda, calling to her as he ran the dozen feet. She waited, her eyes only a little less wild than before. With a hard tug, Wes jerked the robber's boot out from under the fender and the rear rigging and let the body fall to the ground. Matilda didn't move. She looked back at Wes with her big brown eyes. He stepped into the saddle, held the Spencer and dug his boot heels into Matilda's ribs, urging her up the slope toward the pines.

Wes huddled low against Matilda's neck, but no shots came from the woods. He charged into the brush and through it, and around the treasure pine where he had left the money. No one was there. He spotted an abandoned horse twenty yards through the thick timber. Wes got down and walked the area near the front of the brush where the men might have fired from. He found some empty cartridges but no signs of blood. He retrieved the mount and rode a half mile arc around the pines, but found no sign of the other robber.

He was gone. Wes figured he was a gang-type man, brave enough when he had three or four friends to back him up. Now he was alone, his three friends were dead. Wes's guess was that the other robber would take to his saddle now and ride east or west, getting away from the scene of the crime, and thanking his own private guardian angel that he was still alive.

That left the problem of the $20,000.

Wes thought about it as he rode back to his shack. A man could start a small cattle spread with that kind of money. Of course, it wasn't his, it was stolen. That robbery must have ruined a hundred honest, hard-working citizens down in Long Grass. The money should be taken back to them. Still, what a temptation. He didn't have to decide this minute. He'd think about that tomorrow.

Three days later, all was still quiet around the shack. He had taken the robber's private papers and belongings and put them in a small cloth sack. His name evidently was Ambrose J. Southwaite. He had kin in Vermont. He had received the letter in care of General Delivery, Great Falls. So three of the four men who robbed the bank were dead.

Wes would turn over the private goods of the dead man and of the head robber, Liberty, as soon as he went back to the ranch. He had buried Southwaite the next morning, over a ways from his partner in crime.

One point bothered Wes. Had they really killed Tom Swanson? The next day was time to swing to the west on his ride. He left an hour before sunup, hurried through the route to the far end and sat looking at the breaks. Tom had said he'd ride through them to get back to the Slash S. How? Where?

Wes saw what looked like a low pass of sorts in the rocks and upthrusts, and he rode that way. He was a quarter of a mile into the breaks, following a narrow canyon with rocky walls on both sides, when he saw a buzzard flap up from the ground thirty yards up a narrow side canyon.

Wes rode into the gully and stopped at once. To one side lay the wide-brimmed Stetson Tom had worn. In another spot lay the torn and bloody jeans that could have been Tom's. The starkly white bones of a skeleton picked clean were scattered about. Wolves, Wes figured.

He stepped down from his saddle and examined the grisly remains. The checkered shirt was definitely Tom's. A little farther on, he found a belt and a buckle with the initials "TS" on it. Nearby lay a chewed wallet. It held no money, only two letters and some cards with names of musicians on them. Wes took the belt and buckle and the wallet and put them in his saddlebags.

By trading horses with Tom, he'd signed Tom's death warrant. He had no way of knowing that at the time. The two robbers had found him, recognized Liberty's horse and made Tom talk. They either killed him in the process or after they found out all he knew.

One of the bastards had paid for his crime. Wes only wished he'd finished off the second one as well.

On the return ride, he did his chores as a line rider. Found one steer with lump jaw but couldn't get near enough to treat it. He thought of roping it and letting Matilda hold the critter, but the slashing horns discouraged him. Best to have two ropes on a steer that big.

It was nearly dark when he got to the shack, and he found Frisky sitting on the slope behind the shack waiting for him. He threw him a piece of fry bread and watched as the fox sniffed it, tried it, then held it with both paws and ate it delicately, as if he had the whole evening to devour this one piece.

Wes filled out his log, noting the steer with lump jaw, and also recorded finding a body, with the near certainty that it was that of Tom Swanson, 17, son of Zip Swanson of the Slash S Ranch to the west.

Wes slept well that night.

The next day he made his run to the east. He was nearly at the far end of his route when he saw a dust cloud to the south. The more he watched, the more sure he was that it was the Bar-N roundup. They would gather all the animals in that area, then sweep the rest north and send a crew up to push everything south and meet in the middle.

Wes figured the dust clouds were fifteen miles to the south. They would push most of the other stock north and come together ten or twelve miles below Line Shack Twelve. He grinned. They should be sending riders up his way in the morning. By tomorrow night or the next day at the latest, he'd have some chuck wagon food. That is, unless he decided to ride south and meet them.

The next morning, Wes saddled up Matilda and rode south. He saw the clouds of dust on a long line across the grasslands. Two hours along the ride, he came to a pair of Bar-N hands who were yahooing a pair of steers out of some low brush in a wash and heading them south.

"You finally got up here," Wes called.

"Finally? Hell, we're three days early. You working or just strummin' your gitar up here?" The cowboy pointed at a cow and a calf fifty yards over, and Wes spurred Matilda that way and turned the family group south, moving her toward the pair of steers. One of the men kept their small gather heading south, while the other two ranged over five hundred yards of prairie on each side, pulling in the scattered animals to the center and moving them along.

It was slow work. At one place they found fifty head of mixed cows, calves and steers, and they simply drove their twenty head over to the larger group and turned the whole bunch toward the dust cloud to the south where the other riders were bringing in their finds.

It was well past noon before Wes and his two riders had their gather to the central point. They knew where it was because the chuck wagon was there with two barbecues spouting smoke that lifted higher than the dust.

The men ate in shifts whenever they arrived. Wes yelled at some of his friends, waved at Caleb and grabbed a tin plate and knife and fork for a man-sized steak. The cook grinned when he saw Wes.

"How's the hermit up here on Twelve?" the cook asked.

Wes never had known his name. He grinned right back. "Better, now that I get some real cooking again. Steak. Somebody break a steer's leg?"

"Yep. Yesterday, so this one is bled out pretty well." He pointed to the steaks on the grille. "Got them medium and medium-to-well and man-type blood red. What's yours?"

Wes took a medium and piled his plate with scalloped potatoes and the rest of the hungry-man meal. When he finished eating, he went to see Caleb. He didn't say anything about the bank robbers, but he did tell his boss about Tom Swanson.

"I can't be sure this is his belongings or not. But it sure looked like his hat. The belt buckle is right. Figured you might want to take it over to Zip and see what he thought. Sure hope to hell it ain't Tom's. I got to like the young guy."

"Odds are it's his. You said he was heading back home to make peace with his pa. I heard they had squabbles now and then. I'll take a ride over to see Zip after the roundup. Kind of thing a man needs to say in person."

He looked at Wes. "How's it going up here?"

"Fine, so far. The rawhiders spiced up that week a little."

"Found out there was a reward. Sheriff put it in the bank under your name. You're a rich man. I see you helped on the sweep down from the north a ways. We'll finish here tonight and move north near to your shack for cleanup in that area."

Wes thanked Caleb for the reward, then said he'd make himself useful since he was here. He had his lariat, and he went out and helped pull the steers out of the main herd. They cut out the market-ready ones and drove them a quarter of a mile to the side where three punchers kept them bunched.

By four that afternoon, all the market-ready steers had been culled out and checked by the foreman Logan. They would be driven on to the next gather and from there to the next and eventually wind up back at the ranch buildings on a range ready to be driven to market.

Wes rode over to the branding area. A cutting horse drove a yearling without a brand from the herd. Wes moved in and roped the young bull around the head. Another cowboy threw a rear loop, catching both the yearling's back feet.

The two horses backed up slowly until the animal's hind feet were pinched together by the rope, and it fell to one side. Two men ran in quickly. One with the sharp knife castrated the young bull, and a minute later the man with the branding iron pressed the hot iron against hair and hide, holding it just long enough so the hair burned and smoked and the hide was branded deep enough to stay but not all the way through the tough cow skin. The yearling bellowed in rage for a moment, then the ropes were jerked off it, and it scrambled to its feet.

They worked until dark, then Roach Logan yelled, and they all relaxed except the four men assigned to keep the remaining cows and calves and unbranded stock in the herd until morning.

The rest of the crew descended on the chuck wagon for another steak, liver, cow's brains or big slabs of roast beef, whatever they wanted.

There was never any scarcity of food on a roundup. Wes ate his fill, then borrowed a pair of blankets from the cook and unsaddled Matilda. He rubbed her neck and head, patted her on the side the way she liked, then picketed her near the other cowboys' mounts.

He dropped his saddle and lay down on his blankets where he could see the fire someone had built. Wes rested his head on his saddle and pulled the blanket over him, as the night had grown gradually chillier. He shivered, then closed his eyes. He wasn't used to so much work. A moment after he thought that, he was asleep.

Six

The next morning, branding and cutting began at daylight. The fire had been kept going all night by the herders so the irons were hot when the first young steer was thrown. Wes worked at branding for a while, holding the long, hot irons with heavy leather gloves.

He stood with the iron in the fire until the young steer or calf was thrown, then he ran to the spot with the iron, held it against the hip of the animal for the right time and pulled it away. Then he hurried back to the fire to lay the brand end in the flames and red hot coals and grab another iron that was already hot for the next animal.

It was exhausting work, but in a way it was the culmination of a year's labor on a ranch. The owner had a firm count on the number of cows, calves, yearlings, range bulls and feeding out steers as well as how many he'd have to drive to market.

There were two men who watched for any animals which were lame or needed medical attention. The men had their bottles of salve and ointments and roped and held any critter that needed their services. This year there didn't seem to be many sick animals.

They finished the rest of that gather about noon, ate and then the riders fanned out again to pull the stock into another central location. The chuck wagon would be the target point.

Wes rode with a dozen men who went north to work the stock south. They passed his line shack and went four miles deeper into the wilds of the north country, then spread out so they were 200 yards apart and began the sweep south. They found only a couple of dozen animals north of Wes's usual north trail, then worked as a team pushing those and a lot of other cattle to the south.

They did it as before, with three riders moving groups of stock. The two outriders would bring in the cattle, and the third one would drive them south.

By the time they had worked three miles south of the line shack, they could see the other riders pushing animals north. The chuck wagon sat on an open place about six miles from the line shack.

There, Wes studied the gather. He recognized some of the individual animals. One old brood cow with a crooked horn couldn't be missed. She'd tried to hook him with a horn one day when he'd taken an interest in her young calf.

The branding and cutting began again. Wes

pulled out of that work and found Caleb and took him to one side. He told him about the confrontation with Liberty, about killing him and taking his horse and six-gun. Then about the pair of riders who had bushwhacked him and probably killed young Tom Swanson.

"So, we've got a pair of fresh graves up from the Line Shack Twelve," Wes said.

"Any connection with Old Jed getting shot and these three?"

"Don't see how there could be. Happened two weeks apart."

"What about the third robber? Figure he'll come back?" Caleb asked.

"Don't know. One day I figure he will. Next day I decide he won't try without some help."

Caleb stared at Wes for a minute. "Wes, I can't figure these last two men being so all fired determined to get you unless they knew for sure that there was some money involved. Did that first gent have any bank money in his saddlebags?"

Wes stared at the ground for a minute, then nodded. "Yes, sir, he did. I truly haven't figured out what to do with it yet."

"Was it considerable, Wes?"

"Yes, sir, considerable."

Caleb folded his mount's reins in one hand and then let them drop and folded them again as he stared at the branding work. "The sheriff said that bank robbery down in Long Grass hit the town hard. Ruined a whole bunch of folks down there. They was counting heavy on getting that money back, leastwise most of it."

Caleb drew some lines in the dust with his boot toe.

"Wes, whatever you decide to do is strictly up to you. I ain't your pa or your priest. You figure it out. Oh, one small word of advice. The sheriff said something near to thirty thousand dollars was stolen.

"If there's that kind of cash involved, I'd almost for sure count on that one attacker who got away to be coming back. He's got a lot of time and sweat and three dead friends involved in that bank robbery, and he won't just ride away counting lucky that he's alive. Not a chance, so you keep your guard up."

He folded the reins again and let them drop. "Wes, I can't tell you what to do, but I can leave a man with you for a week or so if that would help. I'm being selfish. I'd hate to lose a good line rider."

Wes grinned and nodded. "Don't see that'll be necessary, Mr. Norton. Ain't like they can just bushwhack me and look for the cash. They need me to find where I hid it. I figure I can stand off the last one, or even him and a friend if he can talk one into riding all the way up here. I'll check things careful. Might even sleep up in the brush a night or two just to play it safe."

Caleb Norton frowned and nodded. "Like I say, I can't tell you what to do with that money. Anyway I look at it, it's still stolen cash." He turned abruptly and walked his horse toward the chuck wagon.

The branding finished before dark that night, and the men moved with the chuck wagon to another point on the north rim of the range. They would be about five miles over, and Wes rode with them after checking in at the line shack. All was as it had been before.

Frisky showed up five minutes after Wes did, and he put out some scraps of food for the little fox and watched him eat it. Then he put the nail through the hasp and rode to catch up with the other cowboys before darkness closed in.

It took them another day and a half to sweep the top thirty mile spread of the Bar-N. Then the riders turned south to work down the far western section of the range where it spread out wider and sweep the rest of the Bar-N cattle into their net.

Wes went back to the line shack and found all as he had left it. He had brought up a gunny sack of supplies and food from the chuck wagon the second day. Now he sorted through it and grinned at the fresh things. There was a baked loaf of bread not more than four or five days old, a jar filled with broken eggs, a big slab of bacon and he had brought back two steaks from the cook that morning.

He had steak for supper. He figured it would be a long time before he had steak again. Now it might be a month and a half before he went down for his next resupply.

There was no reason to ride the line for another day or two. The stock would still be bunched and not spread out into its normal graze. He cleaned out the spring again, dug it out more to form a larger pool. Down the trickling stream he dug a new hole to form a water trough for Matilda. He went to the pines and cut down a dead tree.

Using his rope and Matilda, he dragged the log down the slope to the front of the shack. There he worked with the six-foot crosscut saw to turn the pine log into stove lengths. He split them and added the wood to his supply. When the fall days came, it would be cold at night and he might want to keep the fire going longer.

The third day after the roundup, he made a lunch and worked the west side of the range. He spent some time at what he figured were two good spots where Old Jed might have been ambushed. The second one was seven or eight miles from the shack. He rode around some brush and trees on a finger of growth and came to one spot that looked suspicious.

He saw numerous horse droppings as if a mount had been tied there for some time. He stepped down from Matilda and checked the area on foot. Near some brush he noticed some paper trash that could have been sandwich wrappings. He found a half dozen cigarette stubs, and a small, empty matchbox.

There were no shell casings, but a six-gun didn't spit out the brass the way a rifle did. He parted the brush and looked out. The spot commanded the trail Old Jed would have ridden.

He could see the track for a hundred feet each way.

So, he had found the spot where the guard had scared away Old Jed. Now the question he needed an answer to was why?

Wes continued his swing along the top of the Bar-N range. He found no animals that were sick that hadn't been treated a few days before. Nothing seemed unusual or out of place. Near the end of the trail he came close to the box canyon he had found before with evidence of a fire. He rode toward the spot now but wasn't sure where it was.

Twice he rode through the area where he remembered seeing the little valley, but neither time did he see the forty-foot opening that had been there. He moved closer to the side of the hills and examined the area more carefully. About half way along the mile route, he found it. The tip-off were spots of withered branches on some brush. A closer look showed that the brush and small trees had been cut off and leaned against a four-wire fence that had been built across the box canyon's mouth.

The shrubbery concealed any hint of a valley in back of it. The four-strand fence was made to keep cattle in place. He rode closer and peered through the shrubs and branches. The little valley was empty.

He rode away quickly, hoping that no one had seen him. Wes wanted to be the watcher, not the one watched. He finished his run along the north rim of the Bar-N range and came back to a spot where he could see the hidden entrance to the small closed valley. Where could he spend some time unseen, but still be able to watch that spot?

He found it on the side of a small ridge that flowed westward into some real foothills near the breaks where Tom Swanson had met his death. He stepped down from Matilda, tied her to a tree and moved out on the top of the ridge line and bellied down. Yes. By looking past some tall grass and some low brush, he could see the entrance to the valley and a third of the area behind the fence.

He tied his bandanna around Matilda's muzzle so she couldn't open her mouth and make horse talk with any other horses. Then he waited and watched.

He had found the opening about three in the afternoon. By seven-thirty that night and near dark, nothing had happened below. No sign of men or horses or any rustled cattle.

He rode down from the ridge, angling away from the hidden valley and moved quickly along the trail toward the line shack. He decided that he would check the place every two days to see what happened. It had to be a rustling venture, but who would do it way up here, and why hold the cattle there right on the Bar-N range where they could be found?

The brush and trees that concealed the valley must be the answer. If no one could see the valley, they wouldn't find any rustled stock. It was well done. He'd ridden right past the spot twice and not seen it, even though he had been searching for it.

Wes established a new procedure. Instead of riding up to the line shack directly, he made a detour so he could come through the small finger ridge that supported the pine trees. That way he could look over the shack and make sure no strange horse was there, and no small army of bank robbers had camped out and eaten up all of his provisions.

He paused at the end of the trees and checked below. No horses, no smoke from the chimney. He even saw Frisky the red fox prowling about. That was the best sign yet that no one had invaded his line shack.

He rode down, unsaddled Matilda and let her drink from her new pool. The nail was still through the hasp, and no one was inside. He settled down to cooking his supper. He fixed sliced potatoes fried in a skillet in bacon grease mixed with six slices of bacon. He fried the last two fresh eggs from the jar and left the yolks unbroken and then put the potatoes and bacon on top of them.

He thought through his afternoon's work. Someone had used the valley before to hold rustled cattle. Evidently they had to keep a man on the site to keep the cattle in the valley pen. By fencing it, they could eliminate that man's time, and keep him where he was supposed to be, maybe a rider on the Slash S.

The idea made sense. If Tom could ride through the breaks, a determined group of cowboys could drive a small herd of cattle through there. They would bring market-ready steers. But where would they go after that?

He would have to wait and watch some more. So Old Jed must have ridden into the area when they were in the process of bringing in or taking out a herd of rustled cattle. The ground didn't look that cut up the first time he prowled the small valley. Maybe it had been a small bunch, maybe they were simply inspecting the valley and had put out a guard. That would mean they knew a line rider came along this way.

No surprise there. A good rustler had to know everything that went on in a range in order to keep away from riders, line men and roundups.

Wes thought about it until he went to sleep. He was glad to have something new to worry about. He had kicked around the problem of the $20,000 ever since his talk with Mr. Norton. He didn't know what happened to the other $10,000, but figured it could be the bank's way of overstating its loss on general principles. He'd heard of banks and stores doing that before.

He was still confused about the money. It wasn't his, even if he had found it. Captured it might be a better term. A lot of people down in town who had put their money in that bank would be wiped out, left without a penny. People would lose their homes and businesses when they couldn't meet mortgage payments.

Wes squirmed on the rough-built chair. Hell, he could start a good-sized ranch with $20,000.

For half that he could buy fifty good brood cows to start a herd. He could get a homestead and have ten thousand left in the bank.

He dropped on the bunk. He still hadn't found enough grass to make a good mattress. He'd forgotten to ask the cook to find him some ticking. Maybe tomorrow he'd work on more grass. He punched the lumpy gunny sacks and tried to get to sleep.

Wes kept thinking about those men and women in Long Grass who were getting ready to move out of their homes. Damnit! Why couldn't it be simple? Why did he have to get his conscience all worked up?

He went to sleep still worrying about the money.

The next day, Wes rode the east section of his line, found nothing unusual and came home to see Frisky waiting for him. He had crept to within ten feet of the edge of the shack and sat there watching Wes ride in.

Wes tried not to make any sudden moves, and came within six feet of the shy little fox, then moved on by and brought him out some food. The fox sniffed, then ate and looked up for more. Wes tossed the leftover potatoes to the creature. Each time he dropped one, it was closer and closer.

At last he reached out and dropped a slice of potato three feet from his boots. The fox grabbed it, moved back a ways and ate it.

Wes talked softly to Frisky, called him by name and watched him cock his head to one side and stare up at him. Wes grinned and went inside, ready to get his supper.

The next morning, Wes left an hour before sunrise. He had enough food to last two days and his blankets. He rode steadily and made it to his lookout point without using the usual trail. Anyone watching wouldn't have seen him come in. He picketed Matilda, tied her muzzle and apologized for it, then settled down in the weeds and grass to look over the small valley.

At once he saw that something had been changed. The near end of the valley had the fencing swung back with a kind of gate. The fence was attached to a sturdy three-inch thick pole. The pole was then slipped into a wire loop attached to a post at the far end of the fence. Another wire loop went over the top of the pole closing the gate and pulling the wire tight.

Now the gate was open.

Wes figured he was 200 yards from the mouth of the valley. Near enough to see what was going on, but not close enough to identify any of the riders, or to make out their brands.

For a while he saw no one. Then a man left the shade of some trees just inside the gate and wandered through it. He was smoking a cigarette, and Wes could smell the taint on the wind that drifted toward him.

The man looked around to the south and west, saw nothing that caught his attention and meandered back inside. He had a six-gun on his hip and carried a rifle. Wes considered the situation. They opened the gate and posted a man here. Why?

Only one answer, they were rustlers and they had a herd of stolen animals coming in today. Wes wished for a pair of binoculars. With a good pair, he could read the brands on the rustler's horses and on the steers.

It was then about noon. He waited until three that afternoon without any change below. He did see a small fire, for cooking probably, or more likely coffee. Twice more he saw the guard saunter out through the gate and look south and west. Why west?

It was nearly five in the afternoon when he heard the cattle coming. They were bawling like they smelled water. The small stream that wound down through the valley wouldn't water many head of steers for long. This would have to be a quick stop for them. Where would they go from here? A young steer with one broken horn led the pack. Four riders kept the string of animals in line. Wes counted for a time, then lost track. He'd guess about fifty head. They drove the last ones into the pen and closed the gate. Now five riders sat their horses.

Only four men had driven the animals into the pen. The fifth rider must be the guard. They checked the gate one last time, then turned and rode away to the south and west.

One of the five wore a white hat. One of them rode a big palomino that could have been a stallion. Its beautiful golden coat and white mane and tail made the animal a standout. Wes tried to tell who was in charge, but no one man made any motions of leadership.

Wes moved to the other side of the low ridge, where he could see the riders moving away. Still five of them. Now they headed almost due south. Not through the breaks.

So they must not come from the Slash S side of the breaks. Who were they? Damn! he wished he had some field glasses. Next time he got some money ahead, he was going to buy a pair, even if they cost him a whole month's pay.

That was when he remembered that $500 reward money in the bank in his name in Long Grass. He could afford to buy the best pair of binoculars he could find. If only he'd had the glasses today.

He untied the kerchief from Matilda and rubbed her muzzle and her jaw and made her feel better. Then he mounted and rode down through the brush and trees to the gate on the corral. He could see the brands plainly now. Every one he saw was a Bar-N brand. He dismounted and went through the fence and looked at the rest of the cattle. Those in the far end of the pen were all Slash S cattle. It was about half and half. How could they get this many prime steers ready for market off the Bar-N just after the roundup?

Wes rode back to the regular north trail through his long route, so if they did have a lookout in the same place as before, he would go around it. He saw thunderheads building on the open range ahead of him and caught the end of an angry little thunderstorm that left him sprinkled but not wet through.

More than a dozen lightning strikes hit ahead of him, but none came close. He watched the areas as he passed. Sometimes the strikes could start a smoldering fire. He saw none.

He worried the problem all the way back to the line shack. Caleb Norton. Did he know about this rustling? How could something like this go on right under his spurs and he not know about it? Maybe he did know. Then why rustle from himself? Still, someone had rustled Slash S stock and Bar-N steers as well. He couldn't figure it.

When he came near the line shack, he went in through the pines again, but this time didn't see Frisky.

The next day Wes rode the eastern half of his trail. The cattle were still grazing their way north, and he saw few of them. He was back at the line shack early and fed the red fox again. This time it came within two feet of him to pick up food, then scurried away.

Wes went up to the pine tree, looked around, made sure he could see no one, then climbed the pine and checked. The leather bank bag was still there and, inside, the money and the Liberty personal effects. He tied it securely back in place. He came down, picked up an armload of wood and carried it down to the shack.

If anyone were watching, he hoped the wood-gathering ritual would satisfy them. He refused to think about the money. He had a bigger worry on his hands. Rustlers.

Now he was certain that Caleb Norton had nothing to do with the thievery. Still, how could it happen right there on the Bar-N? A dozen ideas came to mind, but he threw out all of them. He simply needed more information.

The next morning he again left an hour before sunrise and rode fast to his lookout spot. He got there a little after noon and tied Matilda's muzzle.

The steers were still there. No one was around. He settled down to wait.

Just before two o'clock, two riders came up from the south, went through the gate and evidently made a count of the cattle. One rider carried a gunny sack filled with something heavy. He deposited it under the brush near the gate. The riders ate something, then mounted and headed back.

They were going south. Wes kicked Matilda in the flanks and sent her slanting down the ridge, then in a wide half circle to bring him into a northward direction. He hoped he hadn't missed the two riders.

Ten minutes later he saw them coming. He stood in his saddle and waved. They didn't notice him. He fired one shot from his six-gun and waved again. This time they returned the gesture and rode toward him.

To Wes's surprise, he recognized the two men. They were both regular working cowboys on the Bar-N.

Seven

Wes knuckled down his surprise and tried to keep his voice normal.

"Curley, Bill. You guys are a long way from home. Sure hope to hell you ain't come to relieve me of my line riding job. I'm starting to like it up here."

Curley laughed. He was a big man with black hair and moustache and a hearty voice.

"Not by a damn sight. Wouldn't have your job for twice the pay. Nope. Bill and me are doing a swing around. Double checking the far ranges to make sure we got everything on the roundup. Seems we get stuck with this job every year. We know the nooks and crannies up in here where them beef can hide."

Wes grinned. "No skin off my shins. Just glad you ain't moving me out. I'm on my west swing along the line. Most of the critters ain't grazed up this far yet after the roundup. You find any that we missed? I thought we combed out this part pretty damn good."

"Nope, Wes. Relax. Ain't found but one or two on the whole damn range so far. Keep telling Roach it's a useless job, but he says it's got to be done."

"Got time to swing by the shack for some food?"

Curley looked at Bill, then they both shook heads. "Can't spare the time. Your shack is eight, ten miles to the east of here. We're heading south. Too far out of the way."

"Well, maybe next time. I better be finishing my run back toward the shack. Not a lot of cattle up here to check on yet, but I got one old cow with lump jaw if I can find her."

They said goodbye and ambled their mounts in opposite directions.

Wes wanted to turn and stare at the two cowboys. They were part of the rustling operation. Curley had been lying through his uppers. That tied the rustling operation to the ranch. But it didn't mean that Caleb Norton knew about it. Caleb was an honest man. Wes remembered how he had cautioned him about the stolen money. Caleb had nothing to do with the rustling, Wes was positive about that. Anyway, why would he rustle his own stock?

Wes worked on it as he rode back toward his line shack. Somebody at the Bar-N was involved. He knew two of them. He just wished he knew who the main culprit was, the leader. Maybe he could watch carefully at the valley and identify some more men. He'd have to be cautious. They shot at Old Jed. On an operation like this, they

106

wouldn't hesitate to kill him if they thought he was on to them.

A hundred head of steers at the railhead would be worth four thousand dollars. Split five ways was eight hundred dollars a man. That was two and a half years of wages for a cowboy.

If they had five hundred head over the course of the summer, that would be twenty thousand dollars, or four thousand per man. Wow! That would be thirteen years of cowboy wages. He could see how the men could fall for a scheme like that. Of course, they must know that they were gambling their lives.

Rustling was a hanging offense in Montana Territory.

As he rode, Wes checked the bandage on his arm. It had given him little trouble since Liberty traded shots with him. He had rebandaged it twice and put some of the salve on it he got back at the ranch.

In another day or two he could leave the bandage off. The round had missed the main muscle, so he didn't have a two-month get-well time with it.

He worried about the rustling. At last he decided that he would check on the canyon every two days. Maybe he could catch them at their rebranding. If they moved the cattle, he had to find out where they took them.

He saw more of the Bar-N cattle now. He was almost a mile south of his usual northern boundary ride. He cut across the range, checking the brood cows now and then and stopping to watch the frolicking of a young calf thoroughly enjoying the carefree life of being two months old.

Something touched his senses. He frowned and looked around. Then he caught a whiff of it. Smoke. He scanned the prairie all around him, then made the circle again. Upwind to the left. He saw the smoke then. One of those lightning strikes had smoldered in wet grass and when the sun at last got it dried out, it took off like a north wind.

He turned and rode toward the fire. It was blowing straight at him. Soon he was in smoke and some ashes. He topped a little rise and below him he saw a concentration of at least two hundred cows, calves and young steers. They were directly in the path of the raging range fire.

He'd seen one once before fry a dozen range steers. He galloped down the slope toward the beef. The only thing he could think of doing was to get between the cattle and the fire and drive them away from it. Maybe at right angles to it so they could get out of the path.

How much time did he have? Distances were so tough to estimate on the open range. He watched the fire as he galloped forward. It was maybe half a mile from the herd.

He might have time. It took him five more minutes to circle the animals and start them moving. He fired his six-gun into the air to get their attention. Then he charged the back cattle, shouting and waving his hat. He didn't care if

108

they stampeded. Anything would be better than letting them stay in the way of the killing fire.

A few of the cows started to move forward. He shot again and screamed at them. He used his lariat like a whip and flailed the cows and young steers, prodding them forward. At last part of the herd began to run. He shouted and waved his hat, and they bellowed and raced away north. He rode hard to the front of about fifty head and turned them to the left. It took him fifteen minutes to get this part of the herd turned and racing away around the end of the fire.

Wes trotted Matilda back to the rest of the herd, another hundred and fifty. It took him longer this time, but he got the whole bunch of cattle moving. The flames were now closer. Some of the old cows smelled the smoke and bawled, at once looking for their calves.

He kept them moving by reloading his Colt and firing six times. The animals walked. Then he prodded them with the rope, screamed at them, waved his hat, hit them with the lariat and screamed some more. At last he got the rest of the critters walking faster. There was no panic this time, no stampede.

He looked behind. The fire gained on them. Would there be time to get the animals out of the way? He decided there wouldn't.

He reloaded the six-gun and lifted his Spencer rifle. This time he bellowed and screamed and waved his hat and fired the six rounds from the handgun and all seven from the Spencer. A few of the older cows bellowed in protest. Then they sniffed the smoke coming at them and slowly they started to hurry, then to trot. Before long all one hundred and fifty head were on a flat-out run away from the flames.

Wes galloped to the front and bent the lead cows to the left again. That was the shortest way to get around the end of the mile-long line of flames racing at them. The wind seemed to die a little, which slowed the fire. It had been whipping up the wind, blowing fire brands ahead and spotting well in advance of the main fire line.

With the herd angled the right way, Wes returned to the back of the cattle and prodded them and shouted until he was hoarse. A few stragglers lagged behind. There was nothing he could do about them.

He shrilled and screamed until the last of the herd had cleared the edge of the line of fire. Wes relaxed and let Matilda slow to a walk and looked behind. They had made it around the end of the wall of flames four feet high with about fifty yards to spare.

He heard a bleating scream and looked at the fire. A cow and her calf stood there, confused which way to run. Then the calf took off, racing directly at the flames. The brood cow bellowed in protest and ran after her offspring.

Then it was too late. The fire whooshed forward, catching the calf and the cow in it. They both must have died quickly, Wes figured. The intense flames would use up all of the oxygen in the area, and the pair would breathe in the heated air and scorch their lungs.

He watched them falter, then stop and soon fall over. The flames licked at their bodies, burned off the hair and their ears and tail, then raced on past.

Wes looked at the area in front of the fire. It had about half a mile to go to a small stream that might stop it. The wind had died down, and that would help.

After the fire burned past them, Wes knew he had to ride the blackened grassland and count any dead cattle. He knew of two. There would be more. He had seen at least one other cow and calf that had straggled behind the herd in its mad dash for safety.

A half hour later the smoke was almost gone. The grass had burned fast, mostly the dead stalks and stems from last year that had not decomposed yet, but once that hot, the flames burned the green grass as well, leaving the prairie naked.

He rode out to the first cow and calf, noted it in his pad of paper and worked back and forth across the burned area for half a mile. He found two more brood cows dead and three calves.

He rode to the one closest to the shack and dismounted. With his belt knife, he hacked off one leg of the cow. He cut in and disjointed it and slung it across the back of his saddle. He could eat off it for two days, and Frisky could work on the rest of the bone and meat for a week.

He turned east after making notes on his log, and rode for the shack. There were more thunderheads growing in the west, moving toward them in the usual weather pattern of west to east. He figured these towering cumulus clouds would not produce rain on him. Maybe farther over to the east.

The wind picked up, but when he looked back at the fire line, he saw that it had burned itself out at the creek. It still had denuded nearly a square mile of range grass. The grass wasn't much of a loss; there was lots more.

The three brood cows were worth at least two hundred dollars each, and the three calves would have meant money down the line. He'd make a complete report for Caleb.

By the time he reached the line shack, it was dark. He called softly and saw a shadow slink around the building. Frisky was waiting for him. He didn't see the fox as he carried the twenty pounds of beef into the cabin. Wes cut off a chunk and took it outside.

Wes called softly. He sat down on the foot-high step and called again. Frisky came up on silent foot pads. His nose twitched, testing the air, catching the scent of raw meat. Wes held out the strip of beef in his hand toward the cautious creature.

The fox moved up almost to the meat, then scurried back. Twice more he nearly took it out of Wes's hand but backed off. The fourth time

112

he came forward with more confidence, grabbed the meat with his jaws and edged back. Four feet away, he dropped to the ground and began eating the fresh meat.

The longer Wes watched the fox in the soft moonlight, the hungrier he became. He eased away from the step and went inside and cut off a slab of the meat and fried it in his big skillet. He took the last can of peaches and opened it, nibbling on the peach slices as the steak fried. He let it get done just right, then pulled it off and dropped it in his tin plate while it was still sizzling.

It was a little tough but tasted great because he was so hungry. He made some more entries in his log book about meeting the two riders, putting down their names and what they had done at the box valley where the rustled cattle were held.

Wes whittled a new point on the wooden pencil when it broke and thought again about the twenty thousand dollars up the slope in the crotch of the pine tree. What in hell was he going to do with it?

The next morning he decided to run the east range. There might have been another fire from those lightning strikes. He fried up two more slabs of beef, wrapped them in paper and took them along for his noon meal.

The run east went quicker than the west one. Nothing to worry about there and few cattle to look for. This side of the range seemed to slow the cattle down. Perhaps they had better graze.

He made his turn around about noon and stopped for his lunch. He had an apple and the fried steak. The meat was cold now but tasted better than anything he'd had all morning. He ate one of them and half the other one, then headed back for the shack.

He came through the pine trees as usual about five o'clock, and when he parted the brush and looked down, he saw two strange horses tied near the shack.

He couldn't see any brands. They were not the same animals that the two Bar-N riders had been on two days ago. As he watched, a man came out of the shack with the two gunny sacks of straw and cut them open with his knife and dumped them out. He went through each part of the dry grass, hunting something.

Wes scowled. The bank robber had come back, evidently with a friend. He wondered if they would ruin all of the food as well. How should he react? If he'd thought in time, he would have shot the bandit when he was outside.

Now he figured he better wait for another such chance. He pulled the Spencer from the boot, loaded in his last full tube of rounds and took a pocket full of loose ones from his saddlebag and bellied down in the brush, where he had a clear shot at the back door of the shack.

He waited a minute, then got up and moved Matilda back over the small rise and out of range of any return fire. He hurried back to his sniper spot and lay down and waited.

Wes decided he couldn't simply kill both of

them from ambush without knowing for sure who they were. He'd have to yell at them, and they'd have a chance to take cover.

It was starting to get dark. One man came out of the shack and went to his horse. Wes tracked him with the Spencer, then bellowed.

"You, at the horse. Hands up. You're covered."

The man whirled, drew his six-gun but saw no target and lunged the eight feet toward the shack's door. Wes fired once, then the man was under cover. Wes didn't know if his round had hit flesh or not. There had been no cry of pain.

What the hell now?

He wasn't about to burn them out of his own living quarters. Shoot their horses? He hated to kill a horse unless it was absolutely necessary. It wasn't yet.

So what could he do?

He kept his rifle aimed at the front door. He knew they could hear him if he called. He'd put one round into the doorframe and tell them they were surrounded by the Long Grass sheriff's posse. That might do it.

"You two in the shack. You're surrounded by the Long Grass sheriff's posse. Come out with your hands over your head."

Wes fired one round into the doorjamb and waited. A rifle poked out the door and fired back. The round sang through the brush ten feet from him, but they knew about where he was.

"You know what we want, bastard," a voice

115

called from the shack. "We ain't leaving until we get it. Might as well make it easy on yourself."

Wes put another round through the door.

In response, they threw the leg of beef out the door into the dirt. Wes scowled. He sent one rifle slug through the broken-out window, hoping he might get lucky. There was no response.

"Come full dark, I'll be out of here and tracking your ass, little man. You'll live maybe twenty minutes."

"Kill me and you'll never find the money," Wes bellowed back at them. He shot again into the frame of the door, sending a shower of wood splinters into the shack.

Darkness would create a problem. He could pull back or try to spot the man coming from the shack. There was a good moon tonight. He settled in with the rifle and sighted on the bottom of the door. The man would try to crawl out in the darkness.

Was there a way out the back of the shack? Wes had explored that chance when he'd been pinned down in there. The back had three feet of dirt behind the thin wall, then slab planks to the roof. No way out except through the door or window, and he could spot both.

When it was fully dark, Wes put a round into the base of the doorjamb. The moon gave plenty of light to see it. He would be able to spot a man coming out.

He did but it didn't help.

Both men charged from the cabin standing

up and darted and dodged to their horses where they stood behind them. Wes got off one shot but was sure he missed.

The robbers began to lead the horses away, using them as shields. Wes swore, then sighted in on the faint head of the closest horse and fired. The animal screamed and went down. The man behind her ran to the left and into the darkness.

As soon as Wes fired, the other horse galloped away into the gloom.

Two men out, one horse. Wes pulled back to Matilda, rode her up the slope into the heavier growth of pines and brush. He'd settle down there. If anyone approached within fifty yards through the trees, he'd hear them at once. Wes didn't plan on getting any sleep that night.

He tied Matilda's muzzle shut with his bandanna. She had looked at him as if asking if this was necessary again. He told her it was and patted her and scratched her between the eyes. She nuzzled him, he hoped in forgiveness.

Wes snorted. Living alone, he was starting to treat his horse like a human being. He shrugged. The living part was what was important right now. If he made just one mistake, he'd be under the torture knives of the two men out there wanting to get rich off stolen money. Damned if he was going to let that happen.

Twice during the night he heard a horse moving through the trees, but it was over a hundred yards away, he figured. He had both the Spencer loaded and an extra tube of rounds with him and his Colt up and ready. He didn't need them.

When daylight came, he figured the two robbers would be back in the shack. That was the important ground, if only because it contained the food supply. They could starve him out, or force him to move away and hunt for a rabbit or pheasant. He wasn't the best hunter in Montana.

When daylight came, Wes moved toward the shack slowly. He darted from one medium-sized pine to the next. Working quietly, checking ahead for any sign of the robbers. He left Matilda where she was tied, but took the neckerchief off her muzzle. She needed water, but he had none for her.

It took him nearly an hour of cautious work to get back to a place where he could see the cabin. He was in a different location now from before. From here he still had brushy cover and could see in the door of the cabin. He found his spot, cleared some weeds from his field of fire, and settled in to wait them out.

The dead horse lay where she had fallen. There was no sign of the second horse. They would protect her since she was their only means of getting out of here.

Wes watched through the door and saw a body move across the opening, then vanish. Good, they were there. Smoke lifted from the chimney a few moments later, and he figured they were frying up the last of the bacon and eating half of his food.

Food didn't worry him now. Staying alive did.

A few minutes later, he saw one of the men belly down at the door and aim up at the spot where Wes had been before. Wes sighted in on the man's torso, and fired. This time there was a wail of anger and pain. The man rolled away from the door. Not a killing shot. One wounded.

Someone barked out words from the doorway.

"Okay, bastard, we'll make a deal with you. Half of it. That's all we want. Won't do none of us any good if we're dead. We'll split the loot with you. Ten thousand for us, ten for you. All you have to do is get it wherever you've hidden it, and leave one of them bundles of twenties on the step here, or throw it down from the brush and we'll go get it.

"You give us half, and we ride out of here and you won't never see us again. Deal?"

"You made a trash heap out of the shack inside?"

"We did some hunting. Didn't make no trash heap."

"How I know you'll leave when you say you will if'n I give you the bundle of twenties?"

"We'll put down our rifles and our six-guns and leave them here on the porch. Then you can follow us for ten miles and make certain we're on our way back to civilization, saloons, whiskey, steak dinners and those lovely, loving female ladies."

The man waited a minute.

"So, you decided? You'll still be a rich cowboy.

119

Leave this hermit's nest and live it up in Wyoming somewhere."

Wes fired a round through the broken window. "No deal," he called when the shot had echoed away. "No deal. You want the cash, you come and get me."

Eight

"You had your chance, you sombitch! You're a dead man, you just don't know it yet. We're coming out right now, and we're gonna run you to tree like some scared old coon. We're the best coon hunters in the whole damned world. You watch us!"

A moment later two men burst from the shack's door, sprinting in zig-zag routes in different directions. Wes fired the moment he saw the men appear and thought he hit one just out of the door, but neither man slowed nor stopped. He levered a new round in, tried to track one of the men, fired, missed, fired again and then the man had vanished behind the shack.

He looked for the second man, but he too was out of sight somewhere. Now the real chase began. They had been smart, both coming out the door at once. He could track only one. Now it was different. They were separated, and he could see both areas. He had the traditional "high ground" in military tactics and could cover either of them coming up that direction.

That meant neither of them would try it. He watched for the man who remained behind the shack. He would have to expose himself to get away from there and have any chance to circle around and come at Wes from the side or even the back through the pine trees.

Also, there was one horse to consider. That animal would give them great mobility in riding to the rear of his position. So where was the horse?

There was a rise that hid the landscape a quarter of a mile to the east. That was where he came over the top of the rise and saw the Line Shack Twelve for the first time. But there were more than 400 yards between the shack and the safe ridgeline on top.

Just then he saw one of the men running away from the shack. He used the same zigzag pattern again. Wes figured his next move and waited for him with his Spencer rifle sights trained on that area.

The runner zagged into his sights, and he fired. He saw the bullet hit the man just as he was starting to turn off that course. It caught him in the middle of the back and drilled him into the dirt and grass of the prairie. He rolled over, lifted his hand and bellowed something Wes couldn't understand, then the arm dropped, and his head rolled to one side.

"One down, one to go," Wes said to himself. He closed his eyes for a moment. How many men had he killed? He didn't want to think about it. His eyes snapped open. If he wasn't alert and careful, the next dead man in this place would be him.

He searched the area to the west of the shack. There was a small ravine there that had been created when the plains periodically received a cloudburst, and the water stormed down any watercourse it could find. It ran south past the shack seventy-five yards. The ravine may at one time have served as a streambed for the seep where his spring was.

Wes watched that small ravine. It was the only place where the second robber could have vanished. He tried to remember it in detail. Yes, it was green on all sides except in the bottom where the rains had gouged out a two-foot deep channel.

A man rolling into that could work downhill on his hands and knees and be out of sight from the pines. He must have gone that way. Chances are the horse would be hidden to the east behind the rise. Over there toward the dead robber.

Problem: did he kill the original robber, or was it the hired shooter the robber brought along to share the money? A hired man might find the horse and ride for home. But if the live one was the fourth robber in the bank holdup, he would fight it out until one of them won.

Another question. Did the robbers both run out the door with rifles, or just one of them? Wes closed his eyes and tried to replay the action as the men surged out the door. Yes, each had a rifle in one hand and a drawn six-gun in the other. So he still had to face a long gun.

Wes looked back at the ravine. It wandered down a ways, and maybe two hundred yards along supported some thin brush that thickened and merged with the same rise of ground where the second man had been headed. The brush was dense enough for the robber to make his escape.

If that was where they had left the horse the night before, the robber would then be mounted and on an equal tactical footing with Wes. What would he do? There would be no gain in riding back to the shack. The robber would think about attacking. How?

Wes studied the land the way a military man might. The area to the south and west lay flat and endless, a sea of grass that stretched a thousand miles to the horizon.

To the east was the low rise of land that cut off his view in that direction after four hundred yards. That rise, which petered out to the south, lifted higher as it worked north and swung a little west until it merged with a finger ridge coming down from the foothills.

Wes nodded. He just might try it. The robber could ride north behind the rise, swing into the pines and the foothills and ride under cover the half mile to where Wes had fired at them from the pine ridge where the treasure tree stood.

Could, but would he? Wes figured he would. So a counter move. Wes left the fringe of brush and ran to where he had left Matilda. He mounted, and, carrying the Spencer, rode cautiously to the east along the ridge. He went through one small valley and up the other side to more pines. Soon he could see where the rise of land merged with the finger ridge. Along there somewhere, the robber could be riding, hoping to surprise Wes where he lay near the treasure tree.

Wes picked his spot. A place where two pines grew close together and he could fire between them. He sat on Matilda behind the trees, ready for any sudden run the outlaw might make. He rested. Wes went over the logic of his move again, considering the terrain. This was the best move for the robber to make.

Twenty minutes later, he grinned as he saw the robber working around some brush and upward into the pines. The victim was riding directly into the trap.

Wes levered a round into the Spencer and aimed through the trees. He'd have the first shot. He had to make it good. He steadied Matilda against the tree and waited.

Five minutes more passed before the horse and rider emerged on the same ridge with Wes. The robber came forward, past some brush and then into the open area between the scattered pines.

At fifty yards, Wes sighted in on the man's chest and fired. Too late he realized he was aiming downhill. The round sailed high and knocked the robber's hat off. He reacted quickly,

125

dropping off his horse, and a moment later he darted back into a tangle of brush and vanished. Wes levered a new round into the chamber and fired where he thought the man was, but he wasn't sure. Matilda pranced a moment, and he lost sight of his target between the trees. He saw the puffs of white smoke from his own two rounds.

Powder smoke was always a hazard. It gave the enemy your exact location. Before he could move, four rifle shots came at him as fast as the man could lever the rounds into place. Wes pushed behind one of the pines and heard two rounds hit the tree.

Then Matilda screamed in agony as she took a bullet through her neck, high up. She shuddered, then collapsed and spilled Wes into the brush and leaf mold of the forest floor.

Matilda rolled to her side and pawed the ground with her front feet in desperation. He heard one of the bones in her front leg crack, and her keening took on a terrible higher note of terror and agony.

Wes felt tears streaming down his face. Nothing could save his mount now. He took out his six-gun and put a bullet through her head, snuffing out her anger and her agony. Wes gritted his teeth, put two rounds in his six-gun, filling all the chambers, and holstered his Colt.

The bastard robber was going to pay for shooting Matilda. It was damn personal now. When he looked out from behind the tree, the horse the outlaw had been riding was gone.

Wes figured they had fled. He took additional rounds from his saddlebags, then worked carefully down to where the outlaw had been. He took no incoming fire. He found the spot where the horse had been, the crushed grass and weeds where the outlaw had been on the ground.

Then the prints of the horse dug deeper into the soft forest mulch as it was mounted. Wes nodded. He'd follow the prints. Even a blind man could make out a trail this easy. He carried the Spencer rifle over his shoulder on the sling and tracked the horse and rider.

The trail continued for two hundred yards, then the horse's tracks seemed to dig less into the ground. The footing could be getting firmer. He tracked the horse across an open space when he saw a faint flash of light off some metal on the hillside fifty yards above him. An ambush! The robber had turned the horse loose, hoping that Wes would follow the tracks of the animal and then the robber could shoot him down.

At once, Wes dove to his right, rolled and came up behind a pine tree just as two shots slammed into the ground where he had been. Wes checked around the tree trunk and saw the spot of the powder smoke. More like forty yards up the slope. He listened. The man had moved to Wes's right to a pine tree. Wes studied it closer and could see an arm extending beyond the tree trunk.

He took careful aim with the Spencer, wedging the rifle against the trunk of the pine and fired.

A scream of pain followed quickly, and the arm vanished from sight. Then Wes heard sounds of the robber running, but he couldn't see him. He was running straight away behind the cover of the pine tree. By the time Wes saw him, he flashed past some other trees and brush and out of sight.

Wes followed. The robber was no woodsman, that was for sure. More like a city man, or at least from some town. Wes stopped and listened. He couldn't see the man, but he was ahead and moving to the right. Wes ran across the angle, hoping to cut him off.

It was still morning. Wes ran from tree to tree now, hoping he was ahead of the man who had turned and was running down the slope back toward the cabin. He must know where the horse would go. Probably it was hit hard and galloped away in fear, but soon it would recover and stop and graze. Where the hell was the horse?

Wes broke out of the pines and brush and knelt down beside the last tree. The horse might go back to water. From here she could smell it at the spring.

A few minutes later, crashing noises came from the woods, and the robber ran out onto the open place thirty yards from Wes.

Wes aimed his Spencer at the man. "Drop your rifle or you're a dead man," Wes shouted.

The robber turned, not believing Wes got ahead of him. He didn't drop his rifle. He quickly pulled it up. Wes fired. His slug went high and left, jolting into the robber's right shoulder, spilling the rifle from his hands.

The robber swore, reached for his six-gun. "Don't," Wes bellowed. He levered a new round forward, but it jammed and the rifle was useless.

The robber saw it and dropped to his knees, picked up the rifle with his good right hand and fired. The round hit ten feet from Wes. Wes pulled his Colt out of leather, but already the robber had lunged back into the brush and trees and there was no target.

Wes ran forward, working on the jammed bullet. He took out his knife and freed it, then threw the cartridge away. He levered the weapon again, and the next round slid into the chamber easily.

Wes ran into the woods fifty feet up from where the robber vanished. He wanted to stay out of good six-gun range. That was the only weapon the robber could fire with accuracy now. He stopped and listened. The man ran forward. Wes charged after him.

After two more stops to listen, Wes figured the robber circled to the north. Maybe he was hoping to lose Wes in the woods.

As Wes tracked the robber by boot prints and sound, he considered letting the man go. Wes could return to the shack, find the living horse and tie it in the pines, then defend the fort.

He rejected the idea at once. The robber could come back anytime, today, tomorrow, next month and kill Wes when he didn't even know he was around. He had to finish it right there, today.

Wes followed again, tracking the boot prints in the soft forest leaf mulch and by an occasional bent-over small tree. He stopped to listen again.

After a half hour, it was plain that the robber had decided to move into the taller timber, upward on the finger ridges and into the real start of the foothills. Wes figured they were a mile from the shack.

He stopped to listen again. Heard a crow high overhead in a tree, then more movement through the otherwise silent woods. Wes worked ahead cautiously. He didn't want to run into another ambush. He'd been lucky before with that sun glint off the robber's rifle.

Twice more he listened, then moved ahead. This time when he stopped he could hear no sounds ahead except the soft wind in the tall pine trees.

He waited for five minutes and heard nothing from ahead. The robber must be down. He could have broken a leg, fallen. Wes moved cautiously, protecting himself every step.

Ahead somewhere he heard a wail of pain. The robber. What had happened to him?

Now Wes moved with more care. Ten minutes later he peered around the side of a two-foot thick pine and saw the robber sprawled over a small pine tree thirty feet ahead.

Wes stared at him. What had happened? The man groaned and seemed to be clutching at his shoulder. Was he only losing a lot of blood? Wes watched for five minutes, and the robber didn't move. Wes stood, swung up his Colt and walked forward.

"Hold it right there," Wes barked. "I've got you under my six-gun and can put six slugs in you so fast you won't know what happened."

"I'm hurt bad," the robber said, pain evident in his voice. "Come help me. Musta broke a damn leg, too."

Wes walked closer, the hammer at full cock on his Colt and the muzzle aimed at the robber's chest. He lay half on his side, his head back, one arm under him. The pine tree evidently bent over when he fell against it.

Wes came closer. He could see no problems.

"You take it easy, and I'll wrap up your wounds and then get you to the county sheriff. He'll be interested in talking to you."

Wes moved closer. He was now ten feet from the robber. He wanted to put a bullet in his heart right then, to end the chase, end his responsibility of a prisoner, but he couldn't.

He stepped closer until he was three feet from the man's feet. In a move that surprised Wes completely, the robber levered off the pine tree and it sprang back to where it had stood for so long. Tied across the front of the small tree was a branch with a half dozen knife-sharp sticks six inches long. They had been sharpened on both ends and one end driven into the branch. It made a deadly kind of swinging dead fall. The tree swished forward.

Wes saw it coming too late. He lunged to one

side away from the sharpened sticks. He almost made it. The end stick in the weapon stabbed into his right arm near his shoulder. He screamed in protest, pulled away from the deadly device and the stick came out cleanly.

Wes held on to the six-gun. He rolled and felt the blast of the robber's hand weapon. He came to his belly and fired his Colt at the blurred figure moving in front of him. The round hit the robber in the thigh and pitched him backwards. His hands flew out, and his revolver slipped from his fingers and landed in the brush.

Wes went to his knees, his Colt centered on the robber's chest. "Give me an excuse to shoot one more time," Wes snarled through his clenched teeth. His right arm hurt like a dozen fires. He couldn't afford to lose much more blood.

The robber was in worse shape. Now he bled from three gunshot wounds, two in his left arm and one in his right thigh. The man held up his hands.

"Can't shoot a man in cold blood. That's murder."

"I could blow your brains out right now for killing my horse. Don't push me. You've done me too much damage. Hell, I think I'll just blast you once more and walk for the shack." He lifted his six-gun, held it at arm's length, and aimed it at the robber's chest. The man wailed and cowered on the ground.

"No. No, please. Don't. Think about it. Make you a cold-blooded killer."

"Like you?" Wes asked, his finger still on the trigger, the muzzle still centered on the robber's chest.

"Yeah, make you just like me."

Wes pulled down the six-gun. "Hell, I wouldn't lower myself to your level. Get on your feet. I'm walking you back to the shack where I'll tie you hand and foot and gag you and then get my bleeding stopped."

Wes got him up and walking. They worked downhill. That was the best Wes could do. He had no clear idea just where they were. He spotted a ravine thirty feet deep and remembered seeing it from the shack. Downhill was the best route here. He ordered the robber to go on down along the side of the ravine. With that as a guide, they wouldn't go in circles.

They had just started down when the robber complained about his right leg.

"Can't walk on it," he yelled. "Hurts too much."

"Then you'll have to crawl. Keep moving."

Half a dozen steps later the robber fell, swearing, screaming about the pain.

"Get up, you're gonna make me cry in a minute."

"Help me up. I can't put that much pressure on this leg. You hit a bone, broke my leg, I swear."

Wes hesitated, then reached down his hand to the man. The robber grabbed his hand, then in a sudden move rolled toward the edge of the ravine and dragged Wes with him and kicked and pushed and smashed him over the side of the thirty-foot drop-off.

Wes flailed his arms, but it was too late. He scraped over the edge, dropped ten feet straight down, hit some sharp rocks and rolled another twenty feet to the bottom of the ravine with the rocks pounding and scraping him all the way.

Wes didn't see the robber above. He heard him running down the hill. Wes sat up, cursing his soft heart. He should have kicked him, not given him a hand.

Wes sat up and checked out his body. His arm had stopped bleeding, but now it began again. He had cuts on both arms, and a spot on his left leg had a bleeding scrape where a rock had torn through his pants.

He tried his arms. Not broken. His legs were sound as well. He stood and checked for his six-gun he had returned to leather. His handgun was gone, but he saw the Spencer where it had fallen ten feet away. He crawled over to it and checked the action. It still worked.

The moment he stood and tried to take a step, Wes realized his troubles were only beginning. He had a sprained right ankle. He tried to take a step on it and bellowed in pain. It wasn't broken, only sprained. He looked around for a stick. Found one four feet long and broke some branches off it. It would have to work.

With the stick for a cane, he worked down the rocky bottom of the ravine. He hoped there wouldn't be a flash flood. Be ironic to drown to death in the plains.

Wes hobbled downstream, and came out in land that he'd seen before. He was about a quarter of a mile east of the line shack, and maybe half that far north of it. The more he walked on the ankle, the better it felt. He hoped he hadn't torn anything in there.

He struck cross country, came out of the brush and trees and could see the line shack four hundred yards ahead. To his surprise, he saw the robber going into the shack. Out front stood his horse with one sack on its back. A moment later the robber came out with a second sack. Food, Wes figured. The robber worked at lashing the sack onto the back of his saddle.

Wes bellied down in the grass and lifted the Spencer. There was no other way. He might shoot all afternoon and never get a clean shot at the robber if he missed the first time. His Spencer wasn't that reliable. He'd never even zeroed it in for long distance shooting.

He settled down and took careful aim. Then he squeezed his finger on the trigger and felt the rifle fire.

Nine

It took him four shots, but the last two put the horse in front of the shack down and dead. He wiped tears away from his eyes. Wes hated to kill a horse, but in this case, again, it was the only way he could prevent the man-killer from getting away. Now, once more, the two of them were on even terms. Almost even. He had a rifle; the robber didn't.

At once Wes realized his mistake. He should have tried two shots to kill the robber. He'd still have had five more to try to take out the horse. Too late, it was done now, and the man he hunted was well out of sight inside the shack.

Again the tables were reversed. Wes wasn't happy about that. Before, he'd put any thoughts of food out of his mind, but now, after a day and a half without any, he was no longer able to suppress the instinct for survival.

All of his food was at the shack. Therefore, he had to go back to the shack, rout the robber out and get something to eat. He moved around the ridgeline until he came to the point where he had first seen the shack. He was four hundred yards from it, but he was looking at the windowless back of the structure the same way he had before.

He wasn't sure if the robber had a weapon. He could have a hideout. His six-gun and rifle were gone, Wes was sure of that. He lifted the fully loaded Spencer and, holding it in both hands in front of him, he moved toward the back of the shack.

Wes expected that at any moment, the robber would step out from the shack with a shotgun and blow him into pieces. What had he done with those three sawed-off shotguns the rawhiders brought? He wasn't sure. Did he bury them with the dead man?

The feeling came to him stronger now that the robber might find one of them and some rounds. That would make him doubly dangerous.

Wes puffed as he came to a stop at the back of the shack. He had not made any noise, and he had not heard anything from the structure. He edged around the wall so he could see the front door. The dead horse lay where she had fallen. He frowned at the memory of having destroyed another horse.

He concentrated on the door. He would slip up on it, surge inside with his Spencer covering the robber, who was probably eating something right now.

Wes moved, jumped through the door and

137

found the robber trying to cut open a can of plums.

"Hold it. Hands in the air. I'm out of patience with you. Do it now."

The robber snorted. Wes shot him in the arm, and he bleated in pain, staggered away from the table, the hunting knife in his right hand.

"Damnit, that's enough!" the robber bellowed. "I can't live this way any longer. I'm starved and I'm shot and I'm hurting. I just want something to eat and some bandages. Then what you do with me is up to you."

"Put down the knife."

"Huh, oh sure. Forgot I had it."

"Put your hands on top of your head. Lace your fingers."

Wes looked around. He saw no shotgun, no weapon of any kind except the knife. He grabbed it with his left hand and pushed the blade under his belt.

"You were going to leave?"

"Hell, yes. I've had enough of you. That money won't do me no good dead."

"So you'd just ride away with half my food, leaving me here with no horse?"

"I was worried about me, not you. You'll make out fine. You got a whole ranch supporting you."

"Turn around and put your hands behind your back," Wes ordered.

The man did so. Wes tied him with some heavy twine. Once he had the robber's hands tied, he told him to sit down on the floor against the wall.

"How about binding up this last hole in my arm. I'm bleeding all over the place here."

Wes nodded, found some rags and tore them into strips and bound up the arm to stop the flow of blood. Then he had the man sit against the wall.

"I'll get us something to eat. I'm as starved as you are. Then we'll talk about what we're going to do. Getting on toward the end of the afternoon. A good night's sleep wouldn't hurt either of us. We'll see. If we have to, we can both walk out of here. It's only thirty miles to the ranch."

"Thirty miles, on foot."

"Been done lots of times."

Wes looked over the food left in the pantry. He brought in the sacks of food the man had tried to steal.

"What's your name?" Wes asked.

"Ethan, Ethan Foster. You gonna tie up the rest of these bullet wounds you put in my hide?"

"None of them killed you, did they? You're lucky." Wes relented, tore some cloth into strips. He made pads from more cloth he had from his gear and tied up the rest of the holes in Foster so he wouldn't bleed all over the shack. Then he tied up his own wounds the best he could.

For supper that night they had lots of boiled potatoes with the skins still on them, an apple and a handful of dried apricots and lots of black coffee.

"Keep us from starving," Wes said. "If I had more time, I could cook some of that new spaghetti stuff. Like noodles except it's different. They got it in dried form now, just boil it for about twenty minutes and put some tomato sauce and stuff over it and it really tastes good."

"Tomorrow," Foster said. "Can I go to sleep now?"

"Soon as I tie up your feet. I don't want you running out on me."

Wes tied Foster's feet together, then ran a rope from his feet through a beam across the roof and knotted it securely. Foster wouldn't be going anywhere. Wes threw a blanket down on the floor for the bank robber. "Stretch out anywhere."

Wes had lit a lamp when it grew dark, and now he found his three blankets on the bare wooden bunk the way he had left them two or three days ago. He couldn't remember how long it had been.

He held the Spencer rifle by his side and lay down on the bunk. Wes used one blanket for a pillow. He'd have to bring up a pillow from the ranch house next time he was down there.

Wes checked the rifle again. Yes, it had a round in the chamber. He eased it back to the bunk and blew out the lamp.

Foster turned over on the floor and groaned once when he hit a bullet wound.

"You still got the money?" Foster asked.

"What makes you think I have it?"

"Liberty had it all. Said we'd meet and split

140

it. Then he took off at night when we were sleeping. We been chasing him ever since. You must have gunned him, cause you had his horse. That means you got his saddlebags and the twenty thousand."

"Still riles you, don't it, Foster?"

"What's that?"

"How your partner in crime ran out on you with all the money."

"Damn right. If you hadn't killed him, one of the three of us would have. Never did trust that bastard. But he did know how to rob banks."

Neither of them spoke for a few minutes.

"So, you still have the money?"

"Might have, might not."

"Not much of an answer."

"I'm the one with the gun, Foster. You're the one with his hands and feet tied and treed to the top rafter. Now get to sleep. I got to figure out in the morning what to do with you."

"Could let me go."

"I could boil myself in scalding oil, too, but don't reckon that I will."

Silence came and for a moment Wes heard the barking of the red fox. Then it faded and the little animal must have wandered off, wondering what had happened to his regular nightly snacks. Wes started to drift off. He came awake suddenly, the rifle in his hands. Then he remembered that Foster was tied hand and foot. There was no possible way that he could get away.

Wes lay there a minute longer, thinking about it. He found a match in his pocket and struck it on the wooden wall. When he held it out, he saw Foster exactly where Wes had left him. He was still tied hand and foot, snoring. Wes grinned and went back to sleep.

Morning came a little after 5:30 that summer day. Wes wasn't sure what to do with his prisoner. About the only idea he'd come up with so far was to walk him the thirty miles back to the ranch, or until he found some Bar-N riders they could double with.

What other choices were there?

He made breakfast. Coffee and oatmeal, but no milk to put on it. Tasted more like mush that way, but it was filling. Wes untied Foster's hands so he could eat. He went to the pantry shelves and when he came back, Foster had a big six-gun in his hand and a grin a prairie-mile wide on his face.

"Tables get turned a little, line rider. Untie my feet before I start punching .45 caliber holes in your legs. I mean right now."

Wes scowled. "Where the hell you. . . ."

"Find this piece?" Foster finished the sentence. "I've hid a weapon or two in my day. You didn't have a spare in your gear, so I guessed you had stashed one around the shack somewhere. Pounded every damn board in the floor until I found the right one.

"I recognized the piece right off. Liberty was damn proud of this Colt. Had it custom-made in Omaha. Cost him more'n two hundred dol-

142

lars. Got real silver inlay on the pearl handles. Shoots damn near like a rifle.

"Now, boy. You and me are gonna find that cash money you stashed, or else you gonna have at least a dozen more bullet holes in you. Oh, you won't die for hours yet. But twelve .45 caliber holes is gonna mess up your body a damn sight."

"A few questions first," Wes said. "You hire that other man you brought with you? Hire him with the promise of a big payday?"

"Sure as hell did. Said he'd get two hundred dollars, cash money for a week's work, gun work. He knew the chances."

"But you never would have paid him, would you? You'd have shot him in the back of the head the first night after you got the bank money."

Foster grinned. "Might just have done that." He took Wes's rifle and emptied it of rounds, then threw it out the door toward the wet seep.

"Won't be needing that anymore."

"Something else. How many people you kill in the bank robbery?"

"Me? None. Two tellers tried to be heroes, went for sawed-off shotguns and got themselves killed. Their own damn fault. Now, you ready to get the money for me?"

"What if I forgot where I put it? That fall down the ravine out there made me hit my head, and I got the forgets."

Foster snorted and brought up the pearl-handled .45. "I'd say that's tough for you, line rider.

'Cause then you gonna be one dead cowboy 'cause he forgot. You want to be dead forgetting something like that?"

"If I'm dead, you damn sure won't find the cash."

Foster shrugged. "Hell, I gave it a good try. I can walk out of here knowing that I tried my best, gave it two tries. It just didn't work for me this time. I'll also know that the sombitch who hid the money won't never be able to give it back or use it hisself. See what I'm saying, line rider?"

Wes frowned. This guy might just be crazy enough to do what he said. But he'd be sure to use up those twelve rounds and punch holes in Wes's legs and arms, anywhere that wouldn't kill him. Wes wished he'd searched the shack better after he tied up Foster.

"So, line rider, what's it gonna be? Do I start my target practice now?" He fired the handgun, aiming between Wes's feet and drilling a hole in the shack's floor boards.

"Oh, damn!" Wes yelped. He thought fast. No sense in getting killed over that damn money. He could pretend to give it up. He might have a chance to jump Foster. He wasn't in the best shape. One lucky crotch kick and the outlaw would be down and screaming in agony. If he ever got the chance.

"Hell, I'm not about to get shot up any more. Got enough holes in my hide now." He looked up at Foster. "That fifty-fifty split offer still good? I hid the money in two places. I'll take you to the first one, give you the ten thousand and then keep the other half for myself."

Foster snorted and took a drink from his coffee cup. "Not a chance. You stashed it in one spot. You ready to walk, or has it been right here in the shack all the time?"

"Not here. That wouldn't have been smart. Outside."

"Let's go."

Foster made him walk in front. Wes moved slowly, trying to think of some way to get the gun away from the robber. He came up with no plan, no idea, not even a dangerous one. Rushing him was no good. The man would shoot him twice before Wes could touch him.

He went toward the spring.

"I need a drink," Wes said.

Foster nodded.

Wes bent and had a drink from the tiny running stream from the seep into the large pool. He still didn't have an idea.

He went on up the side of the rise toward the pines.

"Up there? Up there in the trees?"

"Yeah. Seemed like a safe place."

"Unless you had a forest fire, or a grass fire."

"Didn't."

"So far."

Wes continued up the slope to the trees and pointed to the pine where he put the money. "Up there. I better climb up. That left arm of yours isn't working too well."

Foster watched him for a minute, then shook

his head. "Nope. Not a chance. You're planning something. Maybe get the money and set it on fire or something. Not a chance. I'll go up. You just tell me how high."

Wes had the start of an idea. He let it germinate. "How high? About thirty feet. There's a place where three branches come out of the tree at about the same spot, forming a crotch. The bank bag is tied on the crotch."

"I'll find it. You sit down and stay down. You move around and I'll start shooting. I'm good with one of these short guns, believe me."

He pulled up into the low branches, holding the gun in his right hand. Soon he had to push it in his belt and use his good right hand for climbing. Foster had to crawl around the trunk since the branches were so thick in some places. As he moved up, Wes hunted for what he needed. He found it three steps away.

Wes grabbed the branch and broke off the small twigs. The branch was four feet long and an inch and a half thick at the big end tapering down to about an inch. The small part had been broken off, showing jagged ends.

Wes nodded. He used his pen knife and cut more of a point on the small section. He stopped quickly and turned toward the tree. Foster came out on his side of the trunk again, working upward.

"You found a damn strange place to hide something," Foster called. He was ten feet from the crotch.

"It's up there; I checked two days ago. If you can't do it, come down and I'll go up."

"Shut up and sit down," Foster snapped. Wes grinned and watched the man wince as he tried to use his left arm to lever himself higher. He soon was on the far side of the trunk again. Wes picked up the stick and finished carving the point on the end. At least he had some kind of a weapon. Now he'd figure out what to do with it.

Wes sat there and waited. After the climb up and then back down the tree, Foster would be tired. When he came down to the last branch on the tree he would probably drop off, holding on with his good right hand. That was the time Wes would strike.

Wes heard a whoop from the tree.

"Damnit, you wasn't lying. It's here. Both those beautiful big bundles of twenty-dollar bills. You know how long it would take me to earn this much cash working as a cowboy or even a clerk in town? Hundreds of years. Hundreds."

Wes saw the man lean away from the tree and aim the six-gun. Wes dove to the side and slid behind the trunk of the tree where Foster couldn't see him.

"Don't need you no more, you bastard. You'll get it just as soon as I get down. Even if you run, I'll find you and bury you. Just what you deserve."

Wes heard a cry as Foster lost his grip on a branch next to the trunk and fell three feet through smaller branches. Wes looked around the trunk and saw the robber catch himself with both hands, his face a mask of pain.

"Don't worry, I'm fine and rich and coming to kill you." Wes saw him working around the tree, and Wes moved in the other direction, keeping the trunk between them. When he was close enough to his weapon, he reached out and grabbed his spear and carried it with him as he kept moving around the trunk.

He could run deep into the woods, and he had thought of that, but he needed to stay as close to the man as possible. He had a close-in fighting weapon, so the nearer he could stay to the target, the better.

Foster worked lower. He caught sight of Wes and laughed. "Don't know what you're planning, line rider, but it won't work. I got you by the balls right now. Soon as I get a good shot at you, you're nothing but buzzard breakfast. Nothing I'll enjoy doing more than killing you—except maybe spending all twenty thousand dollars I have in my shirt."

Foster was within eight feet of the ground now. Wes rushed around the trunk again, watching the backside of the man moving slowly down and around.

Wes waited a moment longer, then when he figured he had a chance, he rushed up from behind Foster and swung the heavy end of the spear at his right hand, which held the gun and a branch.

The heavy spear end hit half on the gun butt and half on Foster's hand and he screeched in pain, then in fury as the six-gun slipped from his clutching fingers and fell toward the ground.

Foster let go of the branch at the same time, falling the last six feet toward the ground. Wes had reversed his spear and now thrust it forward, point first, at Foster's falling form. He saw the point meet the body, and he held the stick solidly. He felt it ram backwards, and he held it tighter as it jolted through the outlaw's shirt and penetrated flesh.

A searing scream of pain, frustration and fury blared out in the silent Montana high country. The improvised spear penetrated the soft flesh just below Foster's ribs, continued upward through the side of his left lung and sliced into his heart.

The spear jolted from Wes's hands as the body fell. Foster hit on his back, his good right hand clutching the shaft of the branch spear. He had no time to say a word. His eyes were glassy when Wes rushed up and knelt beside him.

Wes picked up the six-gun and pushed it under his belt. Then he opened the buttons on the dead man's shirt, and took out the two bundles of twenty dollar bills. It must all still be there. Wes trembled, holding it. Twenty thousand! More money than he would ever see again in his lifetime.

Wes sat there a moment looking at the man. Another one he'd killed. But he could summon up no tears. He'd been sadder when he killed the last horse. It had no way of knowing why it died, why it was necessary. Ethan Foster, on the other hand, knew well why he had died, he deserved to. He had killed innocent people, now he was dead himself.

Wes studied the man's face, then stood and walked away. He left the man the way he had died. Perhaps later he could be buried. Perhaps.

He walked to the line shack, hardly knowing how he got there. He sat down and had a long drink of water from the bucket he had brought from the spring that morning. Then he looked at his journal. He'd missed three days of entries. He had a lot to put down.

It was still early in the day. He put the two bundles of money inside his shirt and had another cup of coffee. Now he had a real problem. He leaned back against the wall on the bench that had been built beside the table and laced his hands behind his head.

No. No, he didn't have a problem at all. He knew exactly, precisely what he was going to do. He couldn't ride his lines unless he had a horse. He had to walk back to the ranch and get a horse, no, two horses. One and a spare. At the same time, he would turn over the cash to Caleb or the sheriff, whoever asked for it. He'd give them the whole story from Liberty right on up to Ethan Foster. Then that would be the end of it.

Then he could get back to working as a line rider again. The problem of the rustlers brushed across his mind. There was nothing he could do about it now. He couldn't even tell

Caleb Norton until he was sure who was behind the rustling. If and when he found out.

He stood, found his medical supplies and tried to rebandage his wounds, scrapes, slices and stab wounds. He was a walking medical doctor's patient. He wasn't even sure how many holes he had in his body.

When he had them all tended, he began to get another meal ready. He had lots of dried fruit. He ate that, drank coffee and sacrificed his last can of peaches. The rest of today, he'd rest, then tomorrow, he'd be up with the sun and carrying only his two bundles of bills, Liberty's fancy Colt, and a big lunch, he'd set out to walk to the ranch.

Thirty miles. If he could walk three miles an hour, he could do it in ten hours. He'd leave at five, take a half hour for a noon meal, and with any luck he'd prance into the spread at six o'clock, just in time for supper. At least that was the plan.

Ten

The next day, Wes left the shack on schedule. He wanted to drag the dead horse away where he could bury it, but it would have to wait until he came back with a horse to do the towing. He stopped at the corpse of the hired gunman he'd shot. He turned him over and found some identification in one pocket.

Lamar J. Cartwright. At least he wasn't someone Wes knew. He knew he didn't have time to bury him now, so he walked on. His ankle had snapped back from the sprain. It must have been only a turned ankle with no real stretching of the muscles and cords down in there.

The first few miles went quickly. Then the sun came out with its full summer force, and he took off his wide-brimmed hat and wiped his brow.

It was a longer walk than he had figured. Wes knew he wasn't maintaining his three miles each hour. The familiar landmarks seemed slow in coming.

At noon he stopped and ate a handful of dried apples and some raisins, then had a big drink of water from his canteen. He wasn't sure just how far he had come.

The sun was low in the sky when he saw the familiar low rise he knew was four miles from the home place. It would be dark before he got in. He had blisters on one foot and the makings of more on the other one.

Wes scowled at the damned grass and kept on walking. As his luck had it, there were no long-ranging Bar-N riders returning to the corral. He was too late in the day for that. He had to walk every step to the ranch yard. He continued on to the kitchen door of the ranch house, and Caleb Norton met him there.

"Wes? What the hell you doing down here, and on foot?"

It took Wes a half hour to tell Caleb the whole story about the bank robbers, about Liberty and the other three. When he was done talking, he reached inside his shirt and took out the two stacks of twenty-dollar bills. He dropped them on the table, and Caleb's eyes widened.

"Damn, twenty thousand, I'd guess."

"That's what I counted. The bank must have misjudged how much money they really lost."

Caleb motioned to the cook to bring more food. "I'll doctor you up some on those cuts and scrapes and bullet wounds and such. Then first thing in the morning, we'll ride into town and you can tell your story to the sheriff. Same time we'll turn this money over directly to the bank.

Haven't heard if there was any reward for the bank robbery or not."

It happened that way the next day. They went and talked to the sheriff. He took them directly to the bank, where they gave the bank owner the twenty thousand dollars. He didn't even bother to count it. He peeled off ten of the bills and presented them to Wes as a reward. Wes had him add them to his account at the bank, and the manager grinned.

Back at the sheriff's office, Wes went over the whole story again, gave the sheriff the identification he had on three of the men and said he had no idea who the other one was. Their next of kin would be notified.

The next stop was Doc Gravely, who chuckled at the strange bandages and threw them all away. He treated the cuts and slashes and the bullet hole and the stab wound.

"All of them are going to hurt like fire for the next four or five days. Suggest you stay off your feet, too, until those blisters heal." He had opened the blisters and put some alcohol on them to kill any bad bugs hanging around.

Wes felt better after the doctor's ministrations. They had steak for dinner, and after a beer, they rode back for the Bar-N. Caleb Norton looked pleased.

"Knew I picked the right man to go up there on Twelve," he said. "Didn't know you were going to have all the criminals in the county come up there to visit. I'm happy the way you handled it. Hell, you wouldn't have known what to do with twenty thousand dollars anyway."

They rode along in silence for a few miles. Then Wes had a question.

"About rustling up there. Way I figured it, that would be the last place on the ranch anyone would try to rustle. Of course, I'm keeping my eyes open. We haven't lost any stock up in that area, have we?"

"Hell, Wes. You and Old Jed would know better about that than me. I can't keep track of all the critters up in there."

"Say somebody would try to rustle some cattle from that area. Where could they take them? Not north. To the west are the breaks and some good-sized hills. Then the Slash S is over there, too. They try to bring them south, they run into the other line shacks."

Caleb nodded. "About the size of it. That's why there ain't much use worrying about rustlers up there on Twelve."

Wes couldn't say anything more. He had to be positive who was behind the thieving before he could tell his boss. He had to have proof, catch them in the act.

Wes stayed one more night at the ranch, then picked out a pair of mounts and borrowed a ranch saddle. He used one horse to tie on a sack of new food from the cook, including two loaves of just-baked bread.

Caleb asked if Wes wanted another man to ride up with him and stay a few days until his wounds healed. He snorted and said he could

155

do the job himself, now that he had a horse. Too far to walk the line every day. He waved and rode off. Wes sported a new Colt six-gun in his leather, and two boxes of rounds for the Spencer and the Colt. The Spencer should be all right. It could take rough treatment.

He moved out from the ranch about seven and stopped at midday near a small stream for a sandwich the cook had made for him. Then he rode on to the shack. When he topped the rise in back of Line Shack Twelve, he had the strange feeling of this all happening before. When he looked down at the small structure, he saw smoke spiraling upward from the chimney.

"Oh, no, not again," he said. Wes drew his new Colt and rode down to the back of the shack. He stepped down and went around to the front. Two horses were ground-tied nearby. Wes crept to the door and looked in. Two young men worked over the stove.

He stepped inside the shack and cocked his six-gun at the same time.

"Don't move, either one of you."

The faces turned, showing alarm. Neither of them moved even an eyelash.

"Hey, no need for the pistola. We're friendly. Just got ourselves lost."

The other young man nodded. "Sure as hell did. We was looking for the Slash S, and one bunch of this damn prairie grass looks exactly like the next."

Wes saw that neither of them wore guns. He

156

let the hammer down slowly but kept the weapon in his hand.

"You're thirty miles from the Slash S. Sure you were heading that way?"

"Absolutely. We left Long Grass and somebody must have given us the wrong directions."

Both looked to be in their late teens or early twenties. They might be just what they seemed to be.

"Sorry about charging in here this way. We saw the shack and figured somebody would be here so we could get directions. Then we saw your food, and we got hungry."

The speaker was tall, slender, with short brown hair and a nose too big for his face. He grinned.

"I'm Slim Johnson. Spent most of my life down in Great Falls. Decided to get away from home for a time."

Wes held out his hand. "I'm Wes Parker. I'm the line rider up here on Shack Twelve."

The other young man came forward. He was shorter, a little heavy, with a round face with touches of red in his cheeks, deep-set eyes and black hair. "They call me Harley Dundas. I worked cattle for two years. Like it. Hoped to sign on with the Slash S. Somebody in town said they were hiring."

Wes shook his hand. "What are we having for supper?"

Harley chuckled. "Afraid I'm not much of a cook. I was boiling some potatoes and making coffee."

Wes said he had a better idea. He brought his horse around to the front and unloaded the sack of food, and the two loaves of bread. Inside, he fried some bacon to go with the boiled potatoes, made gravy with the bacon fat and flour and sliced the loaf of bread. He had some crabapple preserves left over and put them out. They had coffee, and Wes wasn't surprised that the three of them put away all of the food, including the whole loaf of bread.

Harley shook his head. "Damn, didn't mean to eat so much, but we ain't had a bite since yesterday noon. Supposed to be a four-hour ride out to the Slash S. That was two days ago."

Slim put down his coffee cup and nodded. "We can do something around here to help make it up to you. Cut wood or something. Know that you don't have a lot of grub up here, and we don't want to eat you into starvation."

By then it was dark outside. The men brought in their blankets and rolled them out on the floor when Wes told them they might as well sleep inside.

Slim sat up. "You got a rifle? If you have, I'll go out in the morning and bring us back a couple of rabbits. Sort of make up for all the food we made vanish."

Wes said that would be fine and blew out the lamp. He kept his six-gun beside him on the wood bunk. Again, he didn't think about ticking or a pillow when he was down at the ranch. Maybe next time.

The following morning, Slim found the

158

Spencer where it had been thrown. He wiped it off, oiled it up and cleaned and refilled the magazine tube through the stock. He asked Wes if it would be all right to go rabbit hunting.

"I'll be careful not to hit any of the stock," Slim said with a big grin.

Harley took the crosscut and the axe and went up to the pines and brought back four armloads of split wood before Wes asked him to stop.

"Got more firewood now than I'll be able to burn up in a year," Wes said.

Slim came back an hour later with two rabbits. He skinned them, turned the hides inside out with the fur inward and put some willow sticks in the hides to keep them stiff while the leather side dried out. He cleaned the rabbits and hung them in the shack to cool out.

Wes explained that he had to ride his fences. The two went along. He told them what he did, how he watched the cattle. Then he told them about the rustlers.

"They have a hidden valley where they hold some stock. Don't know if the steers will still be there by now. We'll take a look. But we have to be quiet in case they have out a guard."

The three of them worked upward to the tree-covered lookout where they could see the gate and about half the little valley. Wes checked it out.

"More cattle there now than before. What I want to do is keep watch on them. Looks like there's only one man on guard duty down there now. We don't want him to know we're up here, so keep it quiet and muzzle your horses. I'd like to check on this place every day, but I can't get over here that often."

"Hell, Slim and I can watch the place. One of us can be here and if we see any action, we'll ride like hell to your shack and bring you back."

Wes pondered it. "I can't pay you anything."

"Hell, for a while just feed us. Set-up like this can't last long. They'll be wanting to get them steers out of there and to market before a week goes by."

"You sure you want to do this? Won't be for more than a week, I'd expect." Wes knew he had extra food. The cook had thrown in more than he needed simply because he came down to the ranch.

Slim and Harley talked a minute, then they nodded.

"Hell, yes, let's try it. Most exciting thing that's happened to us in years."

As they rode away from the spot, Wes made sure that Harley knew the way back to the lookout. He cautioned him that he couldn't have a fire, and he should keep his horse's muzzle tied when he was so close. Harley nodded. He was the more experienced of the two.

"If they bring in any more stock, I want to know. If they start moving out that bunch in there, I want to know at once. Ride like hell."

Harley grinned. "I sure can do that."

Back at the shack, they cut up the rabbits and fried them in the big skillet. The three of them ate both the rabbits. Slim said he'd shoot another one the next day.

Wes packed Harley some tinned goods and half the loaf of bread and some preserves and two small sacks filled with dried fruit. He'd stay two days, then Slim would go out and relieve him. Harley rode off with a wave of one gloved hand.

"Don't worry about me. I can outsmart any rustling bastard I've ever seen."

When Harley was gone, Wes said he needed to check the other side of the range. Slim said he'd go hunting, get another rabbit or maybe a pheasant.

Wes made his sweep around the east side of his section of the big range. The cattle had grazed more to the north now from the roundup. More and more were going across the line and into the five-mile zone up to Canada. He figured before the summer was over, there would be a good number of Bar-N cattle grazing on Canadian grass.

He found one black leg on a young steer. He roped the animal, and his horse kept a constant back pressure on the lariat as Wes walked down the line and treated the yearling's front right leg before he let it go.

Nothing else looked out of the ordinary. He got back to the shack about four that afternoon. This time he was glad to see smoke coming from the chimney. Slim's horse was near the big pool in the spring and picketed.

Wes took care of his mount, a bay mare that

161

knew how to be a cow pony. He put her near his spare mount, a slightly jaded dun he figured would be tough and reliable on a trail drive. There was plenty of water in the trough pool for all three mounts. They drank and then grazed on the grass around the spring and its seep.

Inside Slim greeted him with a wave of a fork. He had a rabbit half-fried in the skillet.

Slim finished turning the meat and put down the fork. "How do you make gravy without milk? Just use the drippings and flour and some water? Will that do it?"

It did. Wes sat down to a real meal, and the first he hadn't cooked in the shack. It was good.

"Wonder how Harley is getting along?" Wes asked.

"Harley? He'll do fine. He's quick and smart. If there's any problem, he'll charge out of there and he won't lead anybody tracking him back here. Don't have to worry none about Harley. He's twice the cowboy and woodsman that I ever will be, but I'm learning."

"You do mighty fine with that rifle. How long did it take you to get the rabbit?"

"About a half hour. Mostly I looked for pheasant, but I never even saw one."

"Best to have a good hunting dog to flush out the pheasants," Wes said. "You can walk within three feet of them, and if they think they're hidden well enough, they won't move and you go right past them."

Slim had a well-worn deck of cards, and they

played poker that night for wooden matches. Wes won the whole stack in an hour, and they decided to get some sleep.

In the dark that night before they went to sleep, Wes couldn't help but ask a question. "Wonder who the hell the rustlers are and how they figure to get a herd out of Bar-N land."

"Easy," Slim said. "Drive them down the far side of the range, pay off one line rider and go out past him into open range, then down to the stock pens at Long Grass."

"Bribe a line rider?" Wes tried to remember who Old Jed said was in the next line shack to the south. He couldn't remember the name.

Slim held up both hands. "Bribing somebody is about the only way they can get the cattle out of your range, I'd say. Maybe they have a better plan. Hope we don't have to find out just what it is."

The next day at noon, Slim decided to go up and relieve Harley instead of waiting for darkness. He took along the same no-cook food that Harley had, without the loaf of bread, and said he'd send Harley back as soon as he got there. Harley should be getting in about eight that evening.

Wes worked on his new saddle, getting it set up the way he liked. He'd thought of finding Matilda and taking his old saddle off her, but it would be a time before he could do that. That was when he realized that the dead horse that he'd left in the yard had been dragged away.

The two visitors must have done that the first day they arrived and before Wes got there.

That reminded him of the man he'd killed east of the shack. He found a spade and went out and found the body. Wes buried him near where he had fallen.

That done, Wes went back to the shack and was pleased when he saw the flash of red and then the perky head of the fox as he came slowly up to the shack.

Wes went inside and found some scraps of food for him and tossed them to him at four feet. Frisky came forward, picked up a crust of the bread and ate it. When Wes talked to the small animal, it sat up and cocked his head to one side.

When the food was gone, the fox slid into the weeds and brush around the spring and vanished.

Wes went back inside and checked his larder. He'd have enough food to feed the three of them for a week, then he'd start running low. The rabbits had helped, and would help again when Slim came down from the lookout. He was pleased now that the pair had come. They could help him keep a full time watch on the rustlers and be ready to move the instant he heard that they were taking the stock out of the valley.

The afternoon drifted away, and Wes had just fired up the stove to think about supper, when he heard hoofs pounding up to the shack. He hurried outside.

Slim slid off his mount, his face angry, tear

tracks cut through a layer of dust down his cheeks. He stood there in front of the shack, unable for a moment to speak.

"They killed Harley. I saw him down the slope soon as I got there. His horse is missing. All the food he had is gone. Looks like they dragged him down the slope and shot him. I got close up to him through the woods without being seen.

"There's twice as many cattle in that little valley as there was two days ago. I saw five or six riders down there around the gate. You better come quick."

Eleven

Wes saddled up and made sure he had the Spencer and plenty of ammunition. He tied two rolled blankets on in back of his saddle. Never could tell when you might need them. Then they hurried out toward the west. Wes made two shortcuts and went a little faster than Slim, whose horse was tired after her hard run. They had to walk the horses every half mile.

Wes didn't think they would ever get there. It was just starting to get dark when they climbed the rise and checked where Harley had been. Wes made sure that no one lay in wait for them. They looked down the slope but saw that Harley's body had been moved, maybe buried.

"What else do you remember about Harley?" Wes asked in whispers. "Had he been roughed up any?"

"A lot. I saw where he'd been branded with a hot iron right though his shirt. Must have hurt like hell."

Wes nodded. "No man can stand that kind of

166

torture without cracking. Which means now the rustlers know about you and me and the line shack. They know we've been watching them. They could have two men watching it from the closest cover, probably the rise with the pines on it just north."

"So what can we do?" Slim asked.

"All we can do now is head back to the shack and see if they are there yet. They won't know exactly where it is. We might get lucky and get there before they do."

A fire flared near the gate below, and they counted four men standing around the blaze.

"You said there were six down there before?" Wes asked.

Slim nodded. He shook his head. "I still can't believe that Harley is dead. Damn! He was a good friend. We did everything together. Even went to school some as kids. Now I talk him into coming out here and this happens."

"Slim, it isn't your fault what happened. It could just as well have been you. Right now, it's our job to get the men who tortured and killed Harley. First, we see if we can get back to the shack. We might be lucky. The bastards might not be able to find the shack in the dark. They'll head for Whitlash Buttes. We've got to see if we can beat them getting back there."

They walked their horses down the slope, then took a different route than they had before and rode cautiously toward the line shack. Wes swept them south, out of the hills and into the prairie, moving west before he turned them south and east.

"They shouldn't expect us from this direction," Wes said. "If they are there, we still might fool them."

Slim shook his head in the moonlight. "I just remembered, all of the food is in the shack."

Wes tightened his jaw. "I've had this problem before. It's not a good one."

They rode through the silvery moonlight. The faint light hitting the grass bounced off and set up a kind of shine that could be seen for thirty yards ahead.

Wes figured they had ridden at least five miles out of their way so they could come up at the shack from the east. It would let them watch it from the rise where he had first seen the place. The four hundred yards range would be within good shooting distance for the Spencer, and he doubted if the riders would think to put a hideout man to the east.

They made it to the rise and both dismounted and bellied up to the top of the earth and looked over. Wes could see no light in the line shack, but there was no window on this side. He saw no horse in the faint distance, but realized in this light there could be a man with a shotgun sitting in back of the structure, and he'd never see him until it was too late.

"What now?" Slim asked.

Wes shook his head. "Wish I knew." They were whispering. Suddenly a horse whinnied down near the shack. Both men jumped to their own mounts and held their mouths closed so the horses couldn't answer the horse talk.

So, there was at least one horse and one man at the shack. That told them something.

Before they could mount, a horse galloped toward them from slightly to the rear and to the north. The air exploded with revolver shots as the rider on the animal fired six times. Wes got out his Colt and flailed four shots at the rider before he turned sharply and rode for the shack.

Wes came up with the Spencer and fired three times at the vanishing blob in the faint moonlight. Then it was gone and the quiet settled over the area again.

A night hawk cried over by the spring.

A coyote serenaded his lady friend a mile away, the sound racing across the distance through the moonlight.

Wes felt something wet on his leg and looked down. Even in the moonlight he could see the blood.

"I been hit," Wes said. Slim hurried up beside him.

"Hurt bad?"

"Hardly felt a thing. I caught one of the rustler's handgun shots. Weird, I didn't feel it until the blood started coming out, and it got all wet down there."

"We best get out of here," Slim said. "We need some brush and trees to get lost in. Which way? To the north up this rise? I remember some brush and trees up that way."

Wes nodded. He stepped into the saddle with

no problem. The hurting would come later. They rode north behind the protective rise of ground to where the brush began, then higher yet as a small finger ridge came down and met the brush. A half mile on, they were in the darkness of the pine woods.

Wes called a halt. "This should put us in a good spot to hide for a while. We better build a small fire and have a look at my leg."

They did. Slim proved to be a good woodsman. He dug back the leaf mold under the pines, found leaves and small sticks to get a blaze going, then lifted Wes's pants leg to check the wound. It was three inches above his boot top in the fleshy part of his leg below his knee.

Wes sweated while Slim checked his leg. Slim shook his head.

"It don't look good. The slug went in your leg, but it didn't come out. We'll have to get it out of there, and the sooner the better. Should we ride for your ranch?"

"Thirty miles over there, through the dark. Don't even know if I could find the way at night."

"It can't stay in there more than a day or two, blood poisoning. Septicemia. My pa's a doctor down in Great Falls. He says it can kill a man in three days."

Wes took a deep breath. "How are you at surgery, Slim?"

"Hey, not me, no, sir. Told my pa I could never do what he does."

"Then go get your pa for me, Slim."

Slim pounded his hand into the ground. "Can't do that, Wes, you know there ain't time."

"Then I guess it's up to you. I got a good knife. You build up the fire a little and get the blade hot and start digging. First tie a gag around my mouth so I won't scream so loud."

A short time later, Wes lay on his side with his left leg on top of his right. The fire blazed up, and Slim pushed the blade of Wes's hunting knife into the coals. When it was hot, he brought it out and used the side of it to cauterize the wound opening.

Wes gritted his teeth. "Get on with it," Wes said through the gag.

Slim wiped sweat off his forehead and probed the tip of the knife into the wound. Wes shivered. Slim probed deeper. Wes gave a little cry, then passed out.

Slim nodded and used his own pen knife to probe deeper until he felt the blade hit metal. He worked the slim blade in farther and began to pry upward. Now he wished he had some of those long-nosed pliers his father used.

He pried and the blade slipped off, then he pried upward again. The bullet moved higher. Four more times the lead slipped off his knife blade before it popped out of the wound.

Slim heated up Wes's hunting knife blade again and seared the open flesh with the hot blade, cauterizing it again, sealing in the blood, and keeping dirt and germs from the wound. Slim wasn't exactly sure what germs were, but

171

his father had always been talking about them. He used alcohol to do the same thing.

Slim tore off part of the tail of his shirt, cut it into strips and bound up the leg wound so it wouldn't break free or get dirty. Now all they could do was hope. He wiped the bullet off and put it in his pocket. Someday maybe he could show it to his father.

Wes came back to consciousness about ten minutes later. Slim had put the fire out and kicked dirt over it. He got their blankets from their saddles and had draped one of them around Wes.

"What the hell?" Wes asked. He felt thoroughly confused. He moved and something stabbed him in the leg. That reminded him of the bullet.

"Is it out?"

"It's out and you're bandaged up."

"Thanks, Doc."

"I put out the fire. Figure we don't want to advertise where we are."

Wes wanted to sleep, but he shook his head and started thinking about the situation again. "Must be two men there. Two were missing from the herd, and we heard one horse from the shack and then another one tried to run us down."

"How long will they keep watch tonight?"

"Hard to tell. They should be on guard duty all night. If not, we might be able to surprise them."

"First thing in the morning, about an hour before sunrise?" Slim asked.

Wes grinned in the moonlight. "Sounds good to me. You may have to do the honors."

"I'd be pleased."

They sat there a minute in the darkness.

"Would it help to put a couple of rifle rounds into the shack to keep them awake longer?"

Wes grunted. "No. Let them think that we ran off, left them here. They'll be pleased that they did what they were told to do. Then maybe they'll sleep better and longer."

Slim grinned in the faint light. "Yeah, I see. Maybe we should move out there a little closer so we can see the place. I figure they'll leave their horses up near the spring. We can get within three hundred yards of the spring and still be in cover."

Wes moved his leg and let out a yelp of honest pain. "Oh, damn. You're right, I'm not going to be waltzing around much on that leg. Yes, let's get mounted and move up closer. First I'd suggest we get their horses and tie them up in the brush or in the pines where they can't see them. Then we might have some surprises for the pair."

They talked about it. Slim helped Wes mount his bay. They worked north slowly, came out into the open once and saw the shack to the west. They went back into the timber and moved another fifty yards north. Slim ran out to the edge of the brush and checked. He came back nodding.

173

"Looks about right. I can work down there to where the horses should be. I can't spot them, but they should be near the spring where they can get some water."

Wes grinned. "Time for you to get down and have some rest. By the star clock up there, it's getting past midnight. I couldn't sleep, not if I tried. I'll be on guard until four a.m."

Slim lay down, though, and slept almost at once. Wes watched the shack below. He dozed, but about four a.m. awoke Slim.

"I'll give you covering fire if they tumble to what you're up to," Wes said. "I hope I don't need to. If you get the horses into the brush, then I'll go back with you to the shack. We might still have some surprises for those two bastards."

Wes lay in the dark at the edge of the brush. He could just make out the shack four hundred yards to the west. He forgot and moved his left leg and wailed softly with pain. The leg hurt more than any wound or damage he'd ever had on his body. He bit his lip and waited out the surge of pain, then relaxed.

He couldn't see Slim. Wes knew that he should have gone along with the tenderfoot. He waited and then waited some more. Just when he was about to give up and start a stumbling walk down the hill, he heard the heavy breathing of the two horses as they walked up the slope toward him.

Slim missed Wes by only thirty yards. Wes

hobbled down to the spot. "I was about to come find you," Wes said.

"Had some trouble with the one horse, she didn't want to come, but I persuaded her with a clout between the eyes." Slim tied the two mounts well back in the brush and out of sight, then they sat on the ridge looking down at the line shack in the faint moonlight.

"What's the star time?" Wes asked. Slim looked up at the the north star and saw how far the Big Dipper had rotated around it. The two pointer stars of the Big Dipper were always aimed at the north star. It traveled around it once every night.

"Getting on toward five a.m.," Slim said. "Be light in a half hour."

"Let's start down. Might take me a few minutes extra."

Wes made it just fine. He found now that the more he walked on the leg, the less it hurt him. It might just be going numb, he wasn't sure. They worked down the slope slowly, careful not to fall and start a slide. At the bottom they cut to the left and crossed the end of the seep from the spring.

Then they stole directly up to the line shack. "They should be coming outside to relieve themselves along about daylight," Wes whispered. "We'll take them one at a time or both together. Remember, they were sent over here to kill both of us."

The two men positioned themselves one on each side of the closed door and waited.

175

After ten minutes, Wes's head began to nod. He straightened up, moved his left leg and the stabbing pain woke him up for good.

About five-thirty, the east crawled with worms of light, then they straightened and stabbed across the dark mantle of night. A few minutes later the light had gobbled up every shred of darkness, and it was dawn.

They heard movement inside. Someone said something but got no answer. Wes stood now beside the door and waited, his Colt in his right hand, poised and ready.

Scuffling sounded from inside, some swearing, then a match flared and someone grabbed the door from the inside. It swung inward, and a black shadow edged into the half light of dawn. The man was tall, with a full, shaggy beard. He turned Wes's way, and at the same time, Slim smashed his six-gun butt down on the man's head. Wes reached out to grab him as he fell, but they both tumbled to the ground.

Wes pulled away from him and stood. Slim came over, and they caught the rustler under the arms and dragged him around to the side of the shack. There Wes tied his hands together, then his feet. Wes took the neckerchief from the man and used it as a gag he tied tightly around the man's head and through his open mouth.

Wes shook his head in disgust. The bearded one was another rider from the Bar-N. His name was Sully something. Hadn't been with Norton more than a few months. Wes gave him an angry kick in the shins and went back to the house.

They waited. It was ten minutes later when they heard movement inside. It was fully light now, and when the second man came through the door he was walking fast and three steps away before Wes called to him.

"Hey, you murdering bastard."

The man whirled, his hand digging for the six-gun that wasn't on his hip. Wes fired a round low, and it sliced through the intruder's thigh and out the other side. The man lunged backwards, fell to his hands and knees and screamed in surprise and pain.

"Welcome to Line Shack Twelve, rustler. Look around good. You won't be seeing much more before you get hung."

Wes knew this one too. Gunner Anderson.

"What's the matter, Anderson? Isn't thirty dollars and food enough for you these days? Caleb Norton's always treated you right. Why you have to go to rustling?"

"No such thing. Me and Sully was up here, and we had to stay overnight and we figured you'd loan us the shack for the night."

"That's why you tried to gun us down when we rode up just before dusk last night?"

"Hell, was that you? Figured it was them damn rawhiders. I don't hold no truck with rawhiders."

"Tell it to the judge, Anderson. Sit down and put your hands behind your back before I shoot you again."

Slim went up behind him and tied his hands, then his feet. Slim stood over him, rage and pain from the loss of a best friend showing plainly on his face.

"You one of the cowards who tortured my friend Harley, ain't you, Anderson?"

"Like I said, we just got up here last night and figured. . . ."

Slim hit him in the face with his fist and tumbled him over into the dirt.

"I should kill both of you right here!" Slim bellowed.

"We'll see that they get the hemp, but it has to be done right and later," Wes said. "Let him lay there. Maybe he'll bleed to death. Now we figure out what to do next." They went inside the shack, and Wes set out some dried fruit and started a fire and boiled some coffee.

"They might send another man over here just to make sure," Slim said.

Wes shook his head. "Doubtful. They probably can't spare any more riders if they want to make a drive soon. Why else would they have six men there? Not just to guard the beef."

They ate their dried fruit and drank the coffee. Then went out and talked to the two men again.

"Anderson, who's behind the rustling?"

"What rustling?. Don't know what the hell you're talking about."

Wes kicked Anderson in the leg just below the bullet wound. Anderson screamed in pain, and he began sobbing. "I don't know. I just follow orders."

Wes started to kick Anderson again, and he screeched for Wes to stop.

"All right, it's Caleb Norton. He gets half his and half from the Slash S, rebrands them and runs them down to the rail head. Doesn't have to share with his partners in the ranch that way."

"Liar!" Wes bellowed. He nudged the bullet hole again and saw that it was bleeding. He didn't care.

The other man proved no more informative. He said he didn't know who was the top man behind it. He just took his orders and was promised two hundred dollars when they sold the steers in Long Grass.

"When is the drive?" Wes asked Sully.

"Hell, soon now. A couple more days, maybe. Unless they get spooked. Had it easy while Old Jed was up here. He never saw nothing beyond the end of his nose."

"Then I came along and messed up the works," Wes said. He went back in the shack and began putting food into a clean flour sack. He took everything they wouldn't have to cook. He had no idea how long they might be gone. Their diet would be heavy on dried fruit and a few canned goods.

They left the two rustlers where they lay. Wes waited for Slim to bring down their horses. The two belonging to the rustlers were left in the woods. They'd be all right for a few days.

"Where are we heading?" Slim asked.

Wes pointed west. "We need to find a new lookout the rustlers don't know about so we can check up on them." They took both the revolvers and rifles from the rustlers and carried them along. A spare rifle or two might come in handy one of these times.

"So when we get there, what happens?" Slim asked.

Wes shook his head. "I don't know. We'll just have to play it the way the cards fall. There's no time to get to the ranch for help now and hope to get back here before they drive the herd away. If they do take them somewhere, we have to follow. If we see that they're heading them to the railhead, we'll have to work up something to send the herd into a stampede. It's about all we have left right now."

Wes winced as he kicked the bay in the flanks. The leg still hurt, but sometimes when he wasn't thinking about it, it didn't hurt quite so much.

"Let's ride, Slim. We've got nine miles and a little bit more before we can find ourselves a lookout."

Twelve

Wes knew the land around Line Shack Twelve well by this time. He took a different route, bypassing the place where Old Jed had been bushwhacked, and winding around so he came out in the small ridges just above the valley where the steers had been held. It was a quarter of a mile from their old lookout where Harley had been caught.

Wes got down from his horse and knew his leg was going to be stiff. He had to walk around a little to get it working right. Then he and Slim moved forward to the edge of the ridge where they could see the valley. It was slightly before midday. They saw four riders around the hiding spot for the steers. Two cowboys served as guards near the fence across the mouth.

A fire burned to one side, and he saw that they had been branding.

"Probably are venting one brand by putting a slant mark through it, and then putting on a trail brand of some kind," Wes said. "Might get them by on a sloppy brand inspector. Or they can always bribe him to take the steers."

"So what can we do now?" Slim asked.

"We can start by hanging those five rustlers down there."

Slim looked up, surprise washing over his face.

"You can really do that? Don't you need a court and a trial and all that?"

"Out on the plains in cattle country, justice is sometimes swift and deadly. I saw a man hanged once, caught with six head of steers he was driving off the range. The owner of the ranch rode out, pronounced sentence and hung the man to a convenient cottonwood. The owner told the sheriff, gave him a report and the man's personal items. The sheriff was satisfied."

"Damn! Hanging a man, just like that. I guess Wild West justice can be sudden."

"So until we hang them, we'll watch them. I'd thought of using our rifles to harass them with sniper fire. But that wouldn't do much good, just make them mad mostly. So we watch. If they start to move the herd, that's when we'll get into action.

"In the meantime, let's count the herd. We should know how many critters these men have stolen."

It came down to more an estimate than a count. Wes figured two hundred and fifty head. Slim came up with two hundred and thirty. They decided they put in the report two hundred and forty. At forty dollars a head, that was still almost ten thousand dollars worth of beef.

Late that afternoon they noticed a change. Below, the riders had spread out in the valley and had herded the steers into a group near the front gate.

"Looks like trailing time," Wes said. "We better get some sleep. Bet they'll be moving the herd out with first light."

They made a cold camp, ate their dried fruit and drank water from their canteens and then went to their bedrolls. They heard almost no noise from the rustlers' camp below.

Wes was up a half hour before daylight. He could see little below, but he could tell by the sounds that the cowboys were up and had breakfast and were getting ready to ride.

With the first hints of dawn, the men below opened the gate and roused the steers, prodding them awake, then moving them out in a line three or four wide and two hundred yards long.

Wes and Slim waited until they figured out the direction of the drive, then they rode down into the edge of the prairie, cut behind the cattle so they would be closest to the breaks, and got ready.

"How was that again?" Slim asked.

"We're going to stampede the herd. We'll come at them from the side shooting our six-guns, screeching and screaming and waving our hats. We'll charge right up to the middle of the herd, trying to scare them into stampeding. Usually it works."

"What about the five rustlers?" Slim asked.

"A couple of good rifle shots should keep them at their distance, at least at first. We want a surprise attack, one that will do the job in one loud charge. If we can get the cattle running to the side, the riders will have their hands full trying to stop the stampede and won't even think about us."

They waited in a brushy spot until they saw the outrider on their side gallop to the rear to help bring three strays back into the line of march. The steers weren't used to moving this way in a line, and the rustlers were having trouble with them.

"Now!" Wes said, and the two men rode hard toward the sides of the cattle a hundred yards away. The last fifty yards they shot their six-guns, screamed and waved their hats, coming up against the walking steers, turning and riding at them again. A few of the steers broke on the opposite side of the line and started running.

Wes worked into the line of animals and shouted and waved his hat and fired the five rounds from his second six-gun, and half the herd at once seemed to panic. They broke to the left, swamped one outrider and raced into the prairie grass. The rest of the cattle saw the move and joined them. In two minutes the whole herd had stampeded to the left, away from the breaks, back into the Bar-N range.

Two rustlers came toward Wes and Slim. Wes put a rifle bullet over their heads, and they shied to one side, then turned and rode after the cattle. Wes knew what they were thinking. If they lost the herd, there wouldn't be any drive to market and no payday.

Wes and Slim faded back into the brush and trees along the gentle rise that led into the breaks.

Slim laughed and pointed. "Look at them critters run. Damn, it'll be two or three miles before they stop. Maybe we should chase them, make them run farther."

Wes shook his head. "Make us easy targets for the rustlers. They've seen us now; they know we're on to them. No sense giving them an easy shot and winding up dead."

Slim snorted. "Hey, I'll go along with that. So what do we do now?"

"We pull back a little more, get some altitude and watch the fun out front."

"They'll be trying to round them up again?"

"About the size of it. Now they have to make a gather, get them back in a bunch and then start their drive all over again."

"But we'll mess it up once more if we can," Slim said. He was grinning, having an exciting time. "Damn, this sure beats working in that store in Great Falls."

"The secret out here is to stay alive," Wes said. That dampened Slim's excitement a little. He watched the progress of the riders. They had at last stopped the flight of the steers and now were trying to bunch them and drive them back toward the hills. It would take them the rest of the day to get the animals gathered into a herd again. Then probably it would be morning before they continued the drive.

"Maybe we can figure out something to do tonight to upset their travel plans," Wes said.

"Steal their horses would be good," Slim said. "A cowboy can't do a trail drive without his horse."

Wes grinned. "Damned fine idea. I like that. We'll either have to be downright sneaky, or charge in about two a.m. and dump the guard they'll have out and chase their horseflesh from here to Missouri."

"Now it's getting fun again," Slim said, his eyes flashing. "I've got a lot more to do to pay back these bastards for killing Harley that way."

They watched the gather continue. About midday they had some more of their trail food of nuts and dried fruit and more water.

At two o'clock by Wes's Waterbury, it was obvious where they would try to hold the cattle until they had them all gathered. It was a little swale about three hundred yards from the base of the small hills that were the start of the breaks. The spot was about a quarter of a mile from where Wes and Slim watched from the brush and a few pine trees.

Wes saw one rider bring back two steers, then ride away to the east, evidently after some more strays.

"Wonder if we could capture that lone rider and put the fear of hanging into him?" Wes asked.

Slim chuckled. "I vote that we give it a try. They have five riders. One at the holding area. Two went more to the west about ten minutes ago. One is far south. Let's go pay a visit on our little friend who went to the east."

They rode a quarter of a mile east and a little north in the brush and trees, then broke out of the cover and moved across the prairie with five hundred yards of grass between them. They would try to bracket the lone rider and talk some sense into him.

It was more than a mile into the prairie before they spotted the rider. He had two steers he pushed forward. They squeezed in on him slowly, not knowing if he had seen them yet or not.

When they were a hundred yards away, he stopped and watched them. Wes and Slim both put rifle shots over the man's head.

"Hold it right there," Wes bellowed. The man turned, now saw Slim and stopped. Both riders galloped toward him then, rifles up and ready. He held up his hands.

Wes didn't know him, so he wasn't a Bar-N rider unless he'd been hired on in the last three weeks.

Wes rode up next to him, took his six-gun from leather and a rifle from his boot. The man looked to Wes to be about twenty-five, had a cowboy face tan and a wide-brimmed hat. His saddle was well worn, and he looked like a top hand.

"Why are you trying to get yourself hanged?" Wes asked.

"What. . . . hanged. . . . I don't. . . . Oh, shit."

187

"About the way it'll go. You ride for the Bar-N?"

"No, no. I got hired in town for a special job."

"You knew it was a rustling job, right?"

"They didn't say nothing about no local outfit I'd heard of." He sighed. "Yeah, I guess I knew it was rustling. Promised me a hundred dollars for a week's riding."

"So you knew it had to be rustling."

"You ever gambled your neck before this way?" Slim asked.

"No, sir. But I was broke and getting hungry. Then this guy came along and said he could hire me. Gave me five dollars before I even went to work, and I ate good for two days. Then I came out here two days ago."

"You have a hand in killing that young rider back by the fenced valley?"

"Oh, no, sir, no, not me. I wasn't nowhere around yet."

Wes sighed. "Damnnit. Now we've got to ride this asshole all the way over to the pine trees to find one big enough to hang him from." He looked up at the rider.

"You have a name?"

"Yeah, Bart Rawlings."

"You just made it up on the run, didn't you?" Wes asked. "Don't matter none. You might have a letter in your pocket. Oh, we can't promise you a quick broken neck. All we got are lariats. They'll do the job, but they strangle you rather than break your neck, way a big hangman's knot does."

"Jesus."

188

"About who you should be talking to about now," Slim said. "We better get him moving."

"Who hired you?" Wes asked.

"Don't know a name. Call him Bush something."

"Was he riding a Bar-N brand horse?"

"Never saw his horse."

"Who is the main man behind this rustling scheme?"

"They never told me. I just do my job and keep quiet."

"Until a rope stretches your neck," Slim said. "I'd say you have a chance to bargain your way out of getting hanged if you put some effort into it."

"Right," Wes said. "Tell us how many men do they have."

"Sure. Have five today. Sometimes six or seven. Two guys went over to guard some line shack."

"Most of these men riding Bar-N stock?"

"All but me."

"You do rebranding. You vented the old brands, right?"

"Yep."

"What trail brand did you use?"

"Put a Bar L on them. But I don't know what it stands for."

"Where you driving this herd?"

"Don't know. I got the feeling it was to another holding area that had more grass. That little valley was cropped down to the nubs."

"Bart, you know the way back to town?"

"Yes, sir, south and then some west."

"Make you a deal. I'll sell you your worthless hide for a rifle and a six-gun. How does that sound?"

"You mean it?"

"If you hightail it for town soon as we let you go."

"Damnation to hell! You can have the iron. I'll skedaddle off this range so fast, you'll never even remember seeing me."

Wes looked at Slim. "What do you think, Slim?"

"I'd say get him out of here. Then we won't have to worry about him. We can't feed him anyway."

Wes looked at the rider. He motioned with his head. "Git." The cowboy sat there a moment, then he nodded and pulled his horse's head around and galloped across the prairie due south.

Wes and Slim watched him go.

"I figured you wouldn't have hanged him, nohow," Slim said, a soft grin spreading across his face.

"You're probably right. We could have scared a year's growth off his whiskers, though. Figure he learned a lesson?"

"Figure so."

They took a wide loop to ride back to the edge of the breaks and into the timber and brush well north of the spot the steers were bunched. Then they rode forward unseen to a place where they could check on the rustlers.

By that time the men had most of the cattle reclaimed and settled down. Two herders kept them bunched, and half of them had gone down for a rest.

"They've only got four riders now," Wes said. "One less to worry about tonight. Let's see if we can get their horses out of there. Like you say, a cowboy without a horse is like a rattler without any fangs."

Wes winced when he stepped down from his horse. His leg hurt more today. It was something he could tolerate, but he wasn't sure it was getting any better. He didn't want to unwrap it and look at the bullet hole. He should just leave it until he could get some professional treatment.

They ate again from their saddlebags. They had stopped at a small stream and filled their canteens and watered the horses on the ride back. Now they spread out their blankets and caught a small afternoon nap.

"We'll be up early in the morning," Wes said. He closed his eyes and wondered how this was going to come out. If they did get a drive going, there would be little he could do but follow them to their destination and then scream at the brand inspector. Since two local brands had been vented with a slanted line, it would be easy to check to see if the cattle had actually been sold to the one bringing them to the railhead.

If it got that far. He was determined to stop the drive long before then. What had the rustler Bart said? Something about he had the idea they were not on a trail drive to market, but that they were just moving them to a place with more grass. If so, that was good news. They might want to get a thousand head before they moved them down to the pens. Maybe.

Wes went to sleep then. It was unusual for him to sleep during daylight. When he woke up, it was dusk. Slim waved at him.

"I did guard duty for you while you slept. Figured it might not be smart for us both to be unconscious. You gonna be awake for a time?"

Wes waved. "Yes, sure. Go ahead and have a nap. I figure we better be on the move a couple hours after dark. I'll try to figure out where they're putting the horses. If we're lucky, they'll be at that little stream that comes down near the herd."

"Think we can get them?"

"Never can tell. They'll have one man riding night herder, and that leaves three mounts. We'll give it a good try."

Wes let Slim sleep till midnight, then roused him, and they packed up and rode down toward the prairie. Wes hadn't been able to tell where the horses had been picketed. It was dark before they all came in, so there was no chance of spotting them.

They rode within a quarter of a mile of the herd and tied their mounts to some brush and moved up on foot. Both had rifles and six-guns. They wanted this to be a silent attack, but they were ready just in case.

Well back from the camp, they heard the horses talking. The sound seemed to come from the creek area. That was past the cooking and campfire the rustlers had built. The fire would also be near where the rustlers had rolled out their blankets.

They swung out a little and came in to where they could see the herd of brown against the prairie grass. They waited. Five minutes later the night rider came walking his mount slowly around the cattle.

When he was halfway around, Wes and Slim walked quietly toward the stream. They found the horses. They were tied and had their saddles off. As silently as they could, they untied the three mounts and started moving away.

The night herder left the animals and came over to the fire for some reason. Halfway there he found Wes and Slim with the horses.

"No, by damn!" he yelled. "We got owlhoots in camp!" the drover bellowed. Slim was closest. He charged straight at the night rider leading the horse. The rider cut between him and the horses, sawing him off the reins and blasting a revolver shot at the scurrying Slim. The shot missed.

On the other side, Wes vaulted on the back of the closest animal he led and kicked it in the flanks, charging straight away from the camp and holding the reins to the second horse.

Wes heard four shots behind him, but none touched him or the two horses with him. He galloped to where they had left their horses and caught both reins. Now he led three horses and rode one bareback. He went straight into the prairie a quarter mile and stopped.

Wes could hear shouting and swearing back

at the rustlers' camp and half a dozen rifle shots. He'd seen Slim get parted from the horse he led, but after that he had no idea what happened to him.

Wes did a poor imitation of a mourning dove. To his surprise he heard another bad mourning dove call to his left. He repeated his call. A few minutes later a shadow emerged from the darkness.

"Wes?" a voice asked.

"Slim, over here. I've got your mount."

Slim ran up, laughing. "Damn, we got two of the three. That ain't bad. Be fun to watch these owlhoots making a cattle drive with just two horses."

"Can be done. They'd have to use the two men on foot to do the drag work and whip along the strays. Isn't like they were making more than about three miles an hour."

They rode back to a safe spot in the trees a mile away from the herd and tied the horses securely. Wes lit a pair of matches and checked the left hip of the two mounts. Both had Bar-N brands.

"Caleb ain't gonna be happy about this," Wes said. "Wonder when we should go tell him?" Wes shook his head. "Damnit, no. We can't talk to him until we're sure who's behind the rustling operation. I know for damn sure that it ain't him."

They made a small camp, felt secure enough to start a modest cooking fire and boil coffee in tin cans.

"Tomorrow?" Slim asked.

"See what happens. If they try to drive the cattle, we can't stop them this time. They'll be watching for another stampede. They'll have the cattle out in the middle of the prairie, a mile from the breaks. No cover for us."

"Any time left to sleep?" Slim asked.

Wes nodded. "You go ahead. I'll keep the first watch. They won't be about to try to find us in the dark. But I'll sit up a while. Looks like it's only a little after two o'clock."

Wes watched the stars a while, then the woods. He was sleepy. Not a chance anyone would be hunting them. He had put the fire out long ago; now even the traces of smoke were gone. Wes stretched out on his blanket and went to sleep.

Slim shook Wes's shoulder just after daylight.

"Wes, wake up Come on, we got work to do. It's the cattle. The whole damn herd of them is gone. Can't see a steer anywhere down that way."

They packed up as quickly as they could. Each led one of the spare horsed down to the open space. They found a small stream and tied the horses securely where they could get to the water and still have some graze. Then they rode up to the spot where the cattle had been bedded down.

The only thing that remained was the smell of steers, and a trail of cattle hooves four animals wide heading to the west and coming closer and closer to the roughest part of the breaks.

Thirteen

They caught up with the herd about four miles out. It was a sorry-looking trail drive. The cattle were bunched six across and in a line not much more than a hundred yards long. Two dusty, swearing cowboys walked behind the herd slashing long sticks at the laggards.

Now and then one of the men on foot had to run to the side to try to bring back a steer that didn't want to follow the leader. Twice while Wes watched, the rider along that side had to gallop out and turn a steer back to the herd.

With multiple jobs for each man to do, the herd moved slowly. Wes figured maybe two miles an hour. Wes and Slim trailed a quarter of a mile behind for a while. It was obvious that the cowboys were angry, but still trying to get the job done.

Wes motioned to Slim, and they rode a wide arc around the small trail drive, coming up in front of them. Wes found a slight depression where they could hide their horses, and they bellied up to the front of it and looked at the on-coming herd. When the front cattle came within six hundred yards of Wes and Slim, the pair started shooting at the horsemen on each side of the front of the herd.

They were too far away for accurate shooting, and Wes said they didn't really have to try to hit the riders. But the rifle rounds slamming into the ground and zinging overhead made the horsemen pause and then let the steers stop. The two rustlers rode together and talked for a minute, then began moving the steers ahead again, but this time both of the riders used their rifles and returned fire, aiming at the puffs of white smoke that gave away the snipers' positions.

The rustlers came closer and closer together, and then one of Wes's rounds evidently hit one of the horses. The rider turned and spurred away toward the back of the herd.

Wes waved to Slim, and they broke off the firing and returned to their horses. They rode to the side and watched the little parade pass them.

"Figured it might slow them down a little," Wes said. "Way out here we really have no way to stop them. No cover. They've worked into the prairie a mile, so there's no place for us to jump out and stampede their cattle.

"Now if we had some half sticks of dynamite, we could get them running so they wouldn't stop for half a day."

Slim took a drink from his canteen and shrugged. "We tried. What can we do now?"

"Not a lot. We'll trail along and see where they take the steers. If that other rider was right, they'll put them in a holding area somewhere close by.

"If I was the main man doing the rustling, I'd be on my way to town to bring back some more riders. They can't make a long drive with two men mounted. They know it. I'm just waiting to see what they do after they get to their next stop."

Wes and Slim paced the slow-moving herd. It was so pathetic that Wes almost wanted to volunteer to go in and help them. The men on foot changed places with the men on horses every two hours.

Shortly after noon, the herd angled in toward the breaks. The canyons and hills behind them were sharper and higher now, making them look impossible to get past.

The two hundred and fifty head were angled directly at the breaks, then sent west a little more to a valley that Wes could see from where he rode a half mile off. He was sure it was a large enough valley to hold these and perhaps more rustled stock. This one had no fence, but the mouth of the valley was little more than two hundred yards across. One mounted man could keep the animals from straying.

The rustlers started a fire and ate. Wes and Slim worked on the last of their trail food. It made Wes wonder what he had back at the shack he could be eating about now.

Shortly after the meal at the small camp near the valley, one of the men mounted and rode away from the group. He moved directly south, then rode more to the southeast. Wes was puzzled. From where they were, the town of Long Grass would be southwest of their position. The only habitation he could think of on a southeast direction was the Bar-N Ranch.

Maybe that's where the rider was heading. Most of the rustlers had been from the Bar-N. Wes still wondered who the brains behind the rustling was. Was it someone from the ranch, or a man in town using one of the ranch people?

Wes and Slim started to follow the man. "We can't let him get away," Wes said. "Let's lay down a barrage of rifle fire. Maybe he'll give himself up."

They stopped moving and both fired at the figure now about five hundred yards off. They had little chance of hitting him. They quit shooting and spurred their mounts as they raced after the rider.

He saw them coming and cut out across the prairie. Wes hoped that his mount didn't step in a gopher hole and break a leg.

Wes found out quickly that his horse was not as fast as Slim's. The tall man raced ahead of him, and soon gained on the other rider. Slim slowed his mount to a walk so he wouldn't use her up or make her come up lame.

Most cow ponies were quarter horses or quarter horse mixes. Few could run at a flat out gallop for more than five hundred yards. Then they needed a breather.

Slim was a hundred yards ahead of Wes now. He let his horse walk for fifty yards, then eased her into a trot and made up some distance before the other man raced ahead again. Slim had been close enough to the man to see his features.

Soon though, he gave up the chase. He had discovered that the other rider had a horse that was stronger and faster than his. Wes caught up with him, and they talked it over.

"He's heading for the ranch. We can't follow him that close. We better get back to the line shack and see if those two rustlers we left tied up have died yet."

They turned due east and a little north and rode toward the shack. With luck they would make it just before dark.

They found both the rustlers hungry and so thirsty they could hardly talk. Wes brought water and let them lick a little at a time, so their systems wouldn't vomit it up. They untied them and took them inside when it got dark.

Slowly they let them drink a little more, and then Wes fried some potatoes and cooked some carrots he had forgotten about and opened a can of peas and one of apricots. Nobody starved, but they all could have eaten more.

When the men could talk, Wes tried to get more information from them about the rustlers. He told them the plight of the group, down to two horses and four men.

The rustlers wouldn't talk. They knew they were in deep trouble and now were simply glad to be alive.

That night, Wes thought about every man he knew at the Bar-N, and he couldn't come up with an idea of who might be the rustler leader. Some of the men he didn't like too well, but most of them were not smart enough to cook up a scheme like this one.

They slept after tying the men hand and foot.

In the morning, Slim rode into the brush and brought back the rustlers' two horses. Both men said they were too sick to sit a saddle.

"Fine, we'll tie you belly down over the saddle," Wes said. "Don't make no matter to me."

The rustlers decided they could sit a saddle after all.

Wes didn't expect any trouble on the way back to the ranch. He and Slim had pulled several teeth from the rustlers' tiger. They were down to one horse on site now, and three men, unless they had a new squad of men back at the Bar-N waiting to sweep into the cattle drive. How many men could the rustler boss promise two hundred dollars to and still make a profit?

They rode much the same route Wes had used several times before. He'd brought along some canned goods and some more of the dried fruit. They stopped about noon for some food and had some water from a small feeder stream heading its way toward the Little Chino River.

"What happens when we ride into the ranch?"

Slim said. "I'm wondering how you'll explain me?"

"Tell the boss exactly what happened. He's a fair man. He'll understand. Right now he owes you at least two months' pay for all the help you've given me on this small matter."

Later that afternoon, Wes began to wonder exactly how he should tell Caleb Norton about the rustling. He shrugged. He'd have to do it straight, exactly the way it happened. He didn't know any other way. There would be no benefit in trying to make it into something it wasn't. The rustlers were working from the ranch buildings, he had slowed but hadn't stopped them, and he didn't have the slightest idea who was behind it all.

That decided, he looked forward to getting to the ranch. About three o'clock they came to some familiar territory. He saw two cow hands working some stock a mile over. Then they went down a slight depression in the prairie. It probably was a roaring river at one time. Before they could start up the other side, a rifle snarled, and one of the rustlers screamed in pain and tried to clutch his shoulder.

"Down!" Wes shouted. He and Slim slid off their horses on the wrong side to put the mounts between them and the rifleman. The sound had come from the right in front of them. Now he saw a drift of white smoke. The two rustlers couldn't leave their saddles.

Wes reached over his horse's back and pulled out his Spencer and sent three shots nipping the top of the ridgeline at six-foot intervals to the left of where he saw the first smoke. A right-handed gunman would usually fire and move, but move to his right. He heard no response from his shots.

Wes caught his mount's reins and urged her ahead. Soon she was trotting, and Wes ran alongside her, keeping her between him and the last known position of the gunman.

No more shots came. They soon made it to the top of the rise, and Wes saw a rider pounding away from the site. He was five hundred yards by the time Wes took his first shot with the Spencer. He fired two more shots and then decided it was little use wasting rounds.

He mounted, realized that he hadn't even felt his wounded leg, and rode back to where the others waited. Slim had checked the shoulder wound on the prisoner and tore off some of the man's shirt to tie up the shoulder.

Then they all rode forward.

"Welcoming committee?" Slim asked.

"He had time enough. He could get back to the ranch, come out here on some normal work and wait for us to blunder into his trap."

"Only he must not have expected four riders," Slim said. "How could he know which one to shoot?"

"His problems are only beginning. Do you think you can pick him out of a bunch of cowboys?"

Slim grinned. "For damn sure. Won't never

forget that face. I don't like folks to take shots at me."

An hour later, they rode into the ranch yard. Caleb Norton waited for them on the kitchen porch. He stood with his fists balled and on his hips. His eyes were angry.

"What the hell you trying to do to me, boy?"

Wes frowned. "Mr. Norton, I have something important to tell you."

"I know what you're going to say. You're gonna try to pawn off on somebody else the blame for some rustling that's been going on up in your section. Can't do that. I know the truth. Somebody already told me about you and how you had this spot all fenced off up there by Line Shack Twelve and rustled not only my steers, but prime beef from the Slant S as well."

Wes dropped off his horse and let the reins trail. His face showed confusion and anger.

"Not true, Mr. Norton. None of it. I come here today to tell you about the rustling. You're right about one thing. These two Bar-N riders are part of the rustling gang, and so are four or five others. We couldn't identify all of them."

"Liar!" Norton shouted. "I've been good to you, boy. I kept you on, I give you a good post, and you repay me by stealing from me."

Slim had stepped from his saddle, and he walked forward.

"Mr. Norton, what you say, ain't a mite of truth in any of it. I been with Wes the past week or more. I can vouch for him. He ain't rustled a single damn steer. We been trying to stop the men from doing just that. So far we find they got about two hundred and fifty head of prime steers in a valley up in the breaks west of the line shack over closer to the Slash S."

"Who the hell are you?" Norton asked.

"I'm Slim Johnson. Me and my friend was trying to find the Slash S, and we stumbled on the line shack, and Wes here gave us some food. So we helped him.

"Damn rustlers killed my partner. Tortured him with a branding iron. Wes didn't have nothing to do with no rustling."

"You say. Why should I believe you? I don't know you. I got my information from a man I've known five years. Trust him like my son. Now what you got to say about that?"

"This man you trust, he been gone for three or four days?"

"Yes, out on the west range doing some work."

"He ride in late yesterday all alone?"

"That he did."

"Mr. Norton, I'll wager you a month's pay that I can tell you who that man was, and that he's the same one who has accused Wes here of being the brains behind this rustling plan."

Norton frowned. "You sound damned sure of yourself."

"When you're right, Mr. Norton, being sure comes easy."

"So who was the man?"

"Don't know his name, but I can pick him out. Your hands eating supper about now?"

They were, and the three of them walked over to the crew's dining room behind the cook shack. Sixteen men sat at long tables and benches eating and making big pots of coffee disappear.

"Sit easy, boys," Norton said when he came in. "Just a little experiment here."

Slim walked down the aisle between the tables looking at each of the men. He came back and nodded.

"I found him. I can tell you who he is."

"Then go ahead, Slim. I still don't believe you."

"The man who accused Wes of being the rustler is really the man who planned the whole thing. He's the man sitting at the near end of that first table, the ugly one with red hair."

Norton jolted backwards. "You mean my foreman, Roach Logan?"

"He's the man I chased away from the stolen cattle yesterday afternoon. Yes, sir. And I'll bet he's the one who lied about Wes being the rustler."

Wes looked at his boss. "Mr. Norton, was it Logan who accused me?"

Norton took a long breath. "Yes, Wes. I'm afraid it was. Logan, how could you do this?"

Logan came up from the table with his Colt in his right fist. "Why? To make a little money. I'll never own my own spread on what you pay me." He backed slowly toward the dining-room door. "Just all of you stay still. Don't reach for iron, or you're dead. But I figure I might as

well take out a couple of you as I'm leaving."
He turned and fired at Wes. The round missed,
and Wes drew and fired. His slug took the red-
haired foreman in the top of the chest, smashing
the big bone from his neck to his shoulder. He
slammed backwards, and his Colt fired once
more when it fell to the floor.

Two cowhands jumped on him and kept him
down and the gun kicked away.

"Oh damn!" Caleb Norton said. "You think
you know a man. You trust him. Then he kicks
you right in the balls and laughs at you suffer-
ing."

He took another long breath. "Wes, you and
Slim come into the office. I'll want you to write
this all out for me, exactly what happened. You
say all of the rustlers are also my hands?"

"All except one they recruited in town. We
caught him and booted him toward town after
scaring him half to death about getting hung."

"Let's get this down on paper. We've got a
ride to take tomorrow that won't be pretty, but
it has to be done. Slim, Slim Johnson you say
your name was? I'd bet you've been a big help
to Wes these past few days."

"I wouldn't be here without Slim. I told him
on the way in that you owe him two months'
wages and a permanent spot on your crew."

"Talk about that later," Norton said. "Let me
get some pencils to sharpen and one of them
yellow pads. Oh, Slim, go up there and take care
of Logan and those other two rustlers you
brought in. There's a lock room at the end of

the feed bins in that first barn that will hold the three of them until we know for sure what to do with them.

"Ask some of the men to help you. When you get them stashed, you come into the office."

Wes talked it out and wrote it down at the same time, starting from the point where he found the ambush that hurt Old Jed, right on through finding the small valley, then spotting the men building the fence and bringing in the beef. He told about circling around and meeting two Bar-N hands, coming from the valley, and right on to the death of Harley and their harassment of the drive and their fire fights at the shack and on the drive.

"So, that's about it. I'd say at least seven of your hands are involved, maybe more."

"How were they figuring to get the steers to market?" Caleb asked.

Slim had come in part way through, and Wes pointed to Slim.

"Well, Mr. Norton, the only way I could figure it was they would bribe one of the line riders, probably the next one down from Wes. Then they could drive the herd through there and get into all that open range beyond and have a straight run into town."

Norton nodded. "Be damned. Never know who you can trust. Logan had me convinced you was the one doing the rustling. It all figured. You had the opportunity. Gawddamnit."

Norton stood. "Figure it's about time you two have some chow. You go ask Cookie what he's got he can put together for you. Not just some leftovers. He should have some steaks in the ice cooler. Eat up. Then get some sleep. We're gonna do some riding tomorrow. We'll also be taking along a good half-inch thick rope."

Wes and Slim talked to Cookie, but he already had a pair of big steaks ready to fry. They ate better that night than they had in days. They got to bed early in the bunkhouse, then changed their minds.

Wes and Slim took their blankets and found a spot down by the river where they bedded down.

"Just got to thinking, maybe Logan had more than those six men working with him," Wes said. "Be simple for one still at the ranch to slip a long thin blade between our ribs as we slept."

Slim chuckled. "Damn glad I'm with you. I just didn't think of that."

They were quiet for a minute. Then Slim spoke up. "Wes, thanks for saying that I'd like to have a permanent riding job with Mr. Norton. I'd like it here. You think he'll give me a job?"

Wes grinned in the dark. He was damn sure that Slim had a job at the Bar-N for as long as he wanted it. But no sense letting Slim off the hook.

"Never can tell, Slim. Just never can tell. See you in the morning."

Breakfast at the Bar-N started at 5:30, and Wes and Slim were the first ones in line. After breakfast, Mr. Norton called the two riders to the kitchen.

"I picked out six men I trust. We'll be riding with the three rustlers tied to their saddle horns. Every man will have a big steak sandwich for dinner, and then we'll eat supper when we get back. Course we'll have a sack of dry food on back of a couple of horses just in case we get hungry.

"We can cut straight across toward the breaks and save some time. About thirty miles? Same as to Line Shack Twelve?"

Wes said should be about the same. They were in the saddle by a little after six, and Caleb Norton led the way on a big black stallion. He set a quick pace. He had Wes on his right and Slim on his left.

"Wes, what will be the best way to attack this bunch? You say there should still be three of them up there?"

"If they haven't run off. I'd say the quickest way is to ride up within rifle range and start shooting. When they see thirteen or fourteen horsemen coming at them, I doubt if they'll put up much fight."

"The thieving bastards better fight. I've got in mind to hang every one of them damned rustlers."

Fourteen

Wes Parker looked up at his boss, Caleb Norton, and frowned as they rode along in the early morning mists toward the breaks.

"Mr. Norton, you really serious about hanging the rustlers? Even Logan?"

Norton snorted. "Logan? By damn, he'll be the first one to feel the hemp. I can't abide cheats and swindlers, especially those who betray my trust in them. Oh, yes, if we do stretch a rope a time or two, you'll be sure to see Roach Logan decorating the lower end of it the first time."

Norton shook his head slowly. How great it would be to be twenty-one again and fresh and vigorous and a lamb among the wolves of the real world. Nobody had ever held your hand out there. Nobody watched out for your best interests. That was the job that you had to do for yourself.

Logan. Damn. He had trusted that son-of-a-bitch for six years. How long had he been siphoning off prime steers? He could do it. He had the connections in town. Sandy Welch, the brands inspector, could be bought for fifty dollars. Christ, how much cash had Logan stolen from him by stealing steers over the years? Say five hundred steers a year. No, he'd miss five hundred. Roach wasn't stupid. He'd only take as many as the owner might not miss. But two-fifty might be about right. If he also got that many from the Slash S each year, that would make the half a thousand.

He calculated quickly in his head. At forty a head, that would make twenty thousand dollars a year. Could that be right? He'd have to check with the banker in Long Grass. A cowhand with money like that would be noticed. Say it cost him five thousand a year in bribes and wages for his hands. Still left him with a nice profit.

The bastard!

Norton turned to Wes. "Go back and bring Logan up here. Him and me got some big talking to do. I want you to listen in. Damn that man."

Wes brought up Logan. His hands were tied to the saddle horn and his feet to the stirrups. He wore a thin expression of hatred when he stared at Wes.

"Boss wants to see you up front," Wes told Logan. Wes took the lead reins from another cowboy and moved Logan up to the right-hand side of the ranch owner. Wes rode on Logan's right side.

"How long?" Norton asked his former ram-rod.

"What the hell difference does it make? You've made up your mind. Nothing I say will change things."

"Could. You have a sick mother or something? Is that why you needed the money?"

"No, Caleb. No sick relative. I just like to have money. I'd never get anywhere on the seventy-five a month you pay me."

"You gamble a little at the saloons?"

"No, damnit, Norton. I told you. I wanted to get some money, and this was the best way I knew how."

"How many steers a year you rustle from me?"

"Don't rightly know."

"Two-fifty?"

"Something like that. Couldn't take too many or you'd figure it out."

"Old Jed?"

"Hell, yes. How you think we ran the operation for five years? Had to get through the line shack guards somehow. Hell, money will buy anybody, even Jed."

Norton hit Logan in the face with the end of his reins, bringing a bloody welt.

"Liar. Never believe anything you say after that. Jed would never betray me that way. You lie."

"Fine. I hate you, too."

"Where's the money, Logan?"

"Gone, most of it. Hell, a good woman cost

money to keep. Clothes and fancy underwear right out of the catalog from San Francisco."

"The bank?"

"Got some in there, maybe ten thousand. Not much left."

Norton started to swing the end of his reins again, but Logan ducked his head to the right and lifted his shoulder.

"Five years, twenty thousand a year. You could have had a hundred thousand dollars saved up."

Logan shrugged. "If'n you say so. Never was too good with figures."

"What name you use at the bank?"

"My own. Told them the money was from a rich uncle who died in New York City and sent me ten thousand every year. Hell, yes, they believed me. They just wanted to use the money."

"Get this bastard out of here," Norton spat. Wes caught the reins and led Logan to the side, then turned him over to the cowboy who had been leading him before.

When Wes got back beside the ranch owner, he saw that Norton was still furious.

Wes tried to ease things a little. "How has Old Jed been? I didn't have time to go see him."

Norton brightened. "He's getting along fine. Doc said another day, and he'd have died sure as toads. Caught him just in time. He's up and around now. Does a lot of checker playing and sits on the front porch. He has a daughter in Ohio I never knew about.

"She's been writing to him asking him to come and live with her. He says he don't want

214

to be a burden. Told me once if he could walk in with five thousand dollars to give his daughter, then he'd go down there in a minute."

"Don't you believe anything Logan said about Old Jed," Wes said.

"Slim was right about needing to get through the line of rider shacks. My guess is he went past the one just below yours. We'll make a check there,"

They rode on in silence.

At noon they stopped near a small stream and ate their large steak sandwiches. The steaks must have weighed nearly a pound and had been cut up and put between half-inch slabs of bread with lots of butter and salt on them. Each man had two of the big sandwiches, and Wes figured one of them would make a meal for him. He wrapped the other one and put it back in his saddlebag.

They moved again after fifteen minutes. Norton lifted the group to a lope, and the horses appreciated the change in pace. Wes knew that the lope was the normal running gait for a horse. He'd seen some that could maintain a six-mile an hour lope for three or four hours without stopping.

He'd heard that's how the war-like Plains Indians had given the army such a tough fight. The little Indian ponies could cover long stretches quickly and leave the army mounts and the one hundred pounds of equipment each cavalryman carried far behind.

Norton talked to Wes again.

"No need to touch on the line shack, is there?"

"Not that I can think of. We've got the two rustlers with us who we captured there. I'd think the quicker we can get to the second valley, the better chance we'll have to catch the other rustlers."

"Four of them still there?"

"No, three. At least there were three when we left."

"Those three, three we have here and one town hire who you chased away. That makes seven. Wonder if he had any more of my men on his pay?"

"Probably never find out now," Wes said.

Norton nodded. "I'll take the six that I have."

They came up close to the second valley in the shank of the afternoon. It was just after four o'clock when Wes suggested they stop and look over the situation.

"You've been here before, Wes," Norton asked. "What would you suggest?"

"They've got a lot of trees and brush in there along the sides where they can hide. They must have seen us coming by now. First they'd think it was Logan coming back with some trail drive help. But when they see so many of us, they'll know better."

"That frontal assault you suggested," Norton said. "Will that work? I'd just as soon not get shot out of my saddle or lose any of my men."

"Be about the best. Then if they don't give up, we'll have to circle around to the brush, send in men on each side and flush them out. Keep two or three men out front to grab them."

Norton grinned. "Wes, you could have been an army general. Let's get our men lined up in a company front here and ride forward."

They did. Wes spread the men out ten yards apart. Told them not to fire until they got the word, and then to fire once every ten seconds or so to keep up a continual barrage. He put the three rustlers in the middle of the line and tied them together so they couldn't ride away far if they tried it.

When they were a half mile from the valley opening, the men were all on line and eager. Only one of the riders was old enough to have been in the Civil War. He scowled when he heard about the plan.

"Hell, I was lucky back then. How I know I won't be the only damn one in this line shot through the gizzard this time?"

Norton told him he didn't know, and he could hang back and guard the prisoners if he wanted to. The cowboy had laughed, said he wouldn't miss a shoot-out like this for fifty dollars.

Wes saw one man run out from some brush and look at the army heading for him. He retreated. When they were three hundred yards from the valley opening, they still hadn't seen anyone else. One horse was tied near a still-smoking cooking fire. One blanket roll lay near the flames.

"I'd think about now, Mr. Norton," Wes said.

"Let's start shooting, the way Wes told you,"

Norton called to the others. He brought up his rifle and fired a shot into the brush near the entrance. The other eight men also fired as the horses walked slowly forward.

Wes used up one tube of ammo and put a new one in his Spencer. They hadn't seen any movement. Then on a bare spot on the hill behind the valley opening, Wes saw a man running.

"On the hill," Wes said. Three men lifted their aim and peppered the area with rounds, but the man got away into the brush.

"Two men go after him," Norton shouted. The two cowboys on that end of the line peeled off and rode up to the valley entrance and slanted up the hill.

"Cease fire!" Norton bellowed. Their rifles went silent.

"I'm going to check the other side," Wes shouted and rode hard into the valley and up the slope to the left. Slim went with him. They stopped just inside the brush and listened. Far ahead they heard something moving through the brush and towards the more open land higher on the ridge.

The two men rode hard. They broke through the brush and found two men staggering forward. They both looked like they had run about as far as they could go. They dropped to the ground gasping and sucking in air to fuel their drained bodies.

Wes put a rifle round over their heads, and they turned and held up their hands.

By the time Wes and Slim herded the two cow-boys down the slope and through the brush to where the rest of the crew waited, the third man had been caught on the other slope. He'd decided to shoot it out with the two riders, and they brought him back over the saddle of one of the horses, a dead rustler.

Norton had the three rustlers from the ranch dismount and kept their hands tied behind them. He lined them up with the two new ones and showed them the body of the dead rustler.

Norton went down the line, asking them how long they had worked for Logan on this rustling business. Two of them said four years, one said five and the last said this was his first time.

Norton stared at them. "Each one of you knew the penalty for rustling in Montana Territory, didn't you?" He waited until he got some response from each of the men. Then he continued.

"Some folks think a rustler needs to have a trial. We're having it right now. All the evidence we need is right there in back of you. All those steers have had their brands vented and a trail drive brand put on a Bar L. Sounds suspiciously like the Bar Logan brand. Which isn't registered if that's any interest to you men."

He paced in front of them. "I tell you about the man seven years ago who figured he'd help himself to some of my Bar-N cattle? He had twenty of them. That was six hundred dollars worth back then. One of my hands saw him drive the steers across our boundary and half-way to town.

"We caught him that night and gave him his choice of the gun or the rope. For some reason he said he'd prefer the rope. Never had liked guns. He didn't even carry a six-gun or rifle."

"Was . . . wasn't he supposed to get a trial?" one of the rustlers asked, his eyes going wild.

"Had one. He was the witness, the accused, and the steers were the evidence. I was the judge and jury. One of my hands was the executioner, hangman to be exact."

"So you hung him," Logan said.

"Damn right. First man I ever hung. It got easier after that. Now, I want each of you men to give your names, your real names, so Wes here can write them down to tell the sheriff. Yes, I'll tell him. We have a working arrangement. I take care of legal matters up in this end of the county, and he handles the problems down there."

"You know our names," Logan said.

"Give me your legal names, right now!" Norton bellowed.

All five of them gave names, first, middle and last. All except Logan who turned away, ignoring the whole affair.

"Now, you men here are the jury. You see who we have caught. They have been rustling cattle from this spread and the Slash S. The evidence is right behind you, about two-hundred and fifty head. Now, I ask each one of you men on trial, did you rustle those cattle?"

Logan blurted a "Damn no," and the other four said they hadn't done it. Logan yelled that Norton had no proof.

"Proof?" Norton thundered. "I've got all the damn proof I need. I hereby find all five of you guilty under the laws of the Territory of Montana of cattle rustling. The sentence is death for each of you. You will be hanged by the neck until dead."

"No!" Logan roared. "You can't do this legal. You know that. It's no less than cold-blooded murder. You kill us, and you're worse than we ever thought to be. You let just one of us drop off a horse to the end of a rope, and you're a murdering bastard."

Norton lunged at Logan and slugged him with a right-handed fist that toppled the man to the ground. He lay there tied and unable to get up.

Norton turned to the other four accused. "Does anyone else have anything to say to this court?"

"A few damn steers ain't worth a man's life," one of the hands said. "You're putting a dollar figure on my life. How much am I worth dead to you, Mr. Norton?"

"Somewhere around a hundred thousand dollars. You want to start paying me back by living?" Norton watched the man, who took a long breath and shook his head. He looked away from Norton then and studied the ground.

Norton stared at the hands again, then at the accused. "Let the sentences be carried out posthaste." Norton went to his horse and brought back the rope. He began the process of tying a hangman's knot with the thirteen loops around the noose. When he had it done to his satisfaction, he called for a horse without a saddle and told two of his hands to boost Roach Logan on its back.

Logan looked down at the ranch owner.

"Norton, you ever heard of a man named Johnny Loach?"

"John Loach. You bet. Knew him twenty years ago. We were best friends."

"Were until you shot him to death."

A strange silence settled down over the group. Everyone seemed to turn and stare at Caleb Norton.

Norton shook his head. "Not what happened at all. How come you know about Johnny Loach?"

"Because I knew you killed him, and I wanted to find the man who shot down my father in cold blood."

"Your father?"

"That's right. You were both about twenty, down in Kansas. The war was just over and the cattle business was getting a start. You and my pa worked on the same little spread. One day you and him had a quick draw contest shooting at cans. He always beat you. Remember that?"

"Johnny Loach's son. Why didn't you tell me?"

"I wanted to get a little revenge before I killed

you. I wanted some of your money. Hell, I wanted all of your money. You without no kin, I figured I might get the place left to me. Then five years ago I decided that was foolish, so I had to take what I could. I did."

"You didn't explain about how your father died."

"You shot him down in cold blood. You both took the rounds out of your six-guns and practiced shooting each other. Only you conveniently forgot one round. That round came late, after my pa declared he'd drawn and fired. You shot late, and you aimed good, and your round went through my pa's chest. He died right there in the dirt." Logan glared at Norton.

"Not the way it happened at all. True, it was an accident. I didn't mean to shoot him. We'd been out that night and drinking a little and on the way home we got to challenging each other. One of us would ride ahead and get off his horse. The other one would ride up and make a challenge.

"We both drew and pulled the trigger at the same time. My gun fired, and I couldn't believe it."

Logan nodded. "Sure, sure. Big mistake. Then you went ahead and kept working for old man Rogers. He liked you and willed his small spread to you. It could just as well have gone to my pa. My mother was young, and she had a hard time raising me. She never asked you for a thing. Then you sold out and moved away, and when I grew up I had a hard time tracking you

223

down. But I finally did. You had everything, 'cause of that little 'accident.' "

Caleb Norton hung his head for a minute, then he looked up. "Some of what you say is true, Roach. But it was an accident; the sheriff and the judge both said so. I didn't even know that Johnny had a son at the time. He never told anyone. If I'd known, I would have raised you as my own.

"That all happened when we both were wild young boys. Now we're grown men, and we have to answer to our decisions and our actions. You chose to steal cattle from me. That's a hanging offense. Don't matter now who you were or weren't. You still hang."

He led the horse into the brush and to a small level place where a pine tree shot up fifty feet. Ten feet off the ground a sturdy limb grew out. Norton threw the rope over the branch, then got on a horse and fitted the noose over Logan's head and tightened it around his neck, with the thirteen loops of the half-inch rope pushed solidly against his neck and side of his head. Norton went over and tied off the end of the rope after pulling it as tight as he could, so there would be as little sag as possible.

One of the hands held the horse while Norton backed away. He looked at Logan sitting backwards on the rump of the horse, his feet and hands tied securely.

"Roach Logan, you stole cattle from me. You committed the crime of rustling. In this territory the punishment is death by hanging. May God have mercy on your soul."

Norton slapped the horse on the rump with a stick. The horse surged forward, and Roach Logan slid off the back of the horse and fell two feet before he hit the end of the rope. The large hangman's knot did its work. It snapped Logan's head to the side suddenly as his weight slammed against the knot. The movement broke Roach Logan's neck and all could hear the sudden crack of the bones.

Logan hung there swinging gently two feet off the ground. His eyes had been closed but now drifted open, staring unseeing. His legs twitched, and his mouth came open, gaping in sudden distortion as the last breath of his life gushed out of his lungs.

Twice more his legs jerked, then Roach Logan's corpse swung gently from the surge forward of the horse.

"Oh, God!" one of the rustlers said and crumpled into unconsciousness.

The second rustler in line started to cry, and a moment later he wet his pants, a dark stain spreading from his fly to his left boot.

Caleb Norton blinked back tears. He slashed them away with his hand but kept looking at the body.

"That is what happens in Montana Territory to cattle rustlers. I hope every man here remembers it." He motioned to one of the cowboys. "Go untie the end of the line from the tree trunk and let him down. I brought a shovel. We'll bury him right here."

Norton turned to the four other rustlers. "Now, which one of you wants to be the next to drop off the ass of a horse and straight into hell?"

Fifteen

Wes watched Roach Logan sitting on the rear of the horse with his hands tied behind his back and the big hangman's knot around his neck, finding it hard to believe. Caleb Norton was going to go right ahead and hang . . . kill . . . this man who had been his trusted friend for eight years. How could he do it? Surely Norton would change his mind.

He watched as Norton went to the tree and evidently tied off the rope to insure the proper hanging. Maybe that was it. He had not tied the rope. He'd slap the horse, and it would jolt away, and Logan would fall but fall all the way to the ground, and he'd be frightened half to death but not hurt one iota. Yes, that must be the punishment Mr. Norton had planned for his foreman.

Logan would never work on the ranch again. He'd be cashiered and sent away with a story that every rancher in the territory would know before a month was out. Logan would have to change his name and the color of his hair and go to Kansas or Texas to find work as a ranch hand.

Wes watched Norton get back on the horse and ride up to where Logan sat backward on the horse. He stared at Logan hard, squarely in the eye, then he took the stick and whacked the rear end of the horse hard.

Logan jolted off the mount and dropped . . . but he didn't fall to the ground. The rope had been tied off. It had held. Wes turned away when he heard the hangman's knot break Roach Logan's neck. He knew it was true then. He'd just seen a man hanged.

He turned back and watched the body twitching, heard the last breath come out of Logan and his eyes blink open and his mouth distort in one last terrible grimace. Then it was over, and Logan hung there with only a gentle swaying from the motion of the horse.

A man had died. Wes had seen a man hanged. He had been alive a minute before. Now Roach Logan was dead.

He quailed when Norton looked at the others in line and the two rustlers who had fainted and asked the question about who wanted to be next to hit the end of the rope and die.

Wes lifted his hand to get Norton's attention, but the ranch owner wouldn't look at him. He stepped down from the horse and nudged with his toe the two men who had fainted.

"Wes, splash some water from your canteen

on them. We can't have them missing the rest of the party."

Wes moved forward as if his knees were stiff. He opened his canteen and poured water on the faces of the two cowboys. Both of them gasped and yelped and scuttered away from the water as much as they were able.

When they were fully aware of the situation again, one of them began to cry.

"Stand up like men, you sniveling cowards," Norton barked at them. "At least pretend that you're men. You committed a crime, some of you many times. Now is the time you answer to those crimes. You saw Roach Logan meet his maker. By now he's probably shoveling coal in the furnaces of hell. That's where he's put all of you, right into hell.

"You, Darian. You've been with me five years. Why the hell did you cheat on me this way?"

The cowboy named Darian shrugged. "Can always use some extra money. Money, yeah, that's it. Money for poker, money for the whores on Saturday night. What the hell else I got to do?"

"You risked you life for two hundred dollars?"

"Yeah, why not?"

Norton moved on to the second man. "Curley, two years at least you've been riding Bar-N stock. Why did you stab me in the back this way?"

"My own place, in Oregon. Remember, I told you I wanted a little place on the coast. Been saving money for a long time. Another two hundred a year. That's a lot of money for me."

"Now you're going to hang because of it?"

"For me, Mr. Norton, it was the only way."

Norton stared at the tall, slender man beside Curley. "Bill, what excuse do you have? How old are you, twenty-three?"

"Twenty-four, Mr. Norton. I was bored. I can do all the cowboy things. I wanted more. This sounded exciting, and the little girl in town said for twenty dollars she would. . . ." He stopped and took a deep breath and looked around. "Hell, right now that don't seem like it's all so damn important."

Norton shook his head. He tossed the shovel to one of the men. "Right over there. I want you to start digging. Wes, cut him loose. They'll take turns digging graves. We need two right now, before long that number might go up to six. Just deep enough so the coyotes don't dig them up," he said.

Norton talked to his loyal cowboys. "We need to sort out the Bar-N beef from the Slant S. Put them in two gathers, and then we'll figure out what to do next."

"How'd they get the Slant S steers through the breaks," a cowboy named Friday asked.

"There's two or three ways through. I used to know them all. Think I still remember one. We might need it. Get sorting out that stock; we don't have a hell of a lot of daylight left."

An hour later the four live rustlers had traded off with the shovel and dug two graves three feet deep. Wes had them wrap Logan in his blanket and lower him into the grave. Then the men took turns filling it in.

They did the same thing with the rustler who tried to shoot it out on the hillside. By the time the graves were done, it was dusk.

Caleb Norton rode up from where he'd been helping sort out the steers. The four rustlers sat on the ground near the graves. Wes had tied their hands again with their bootlaces.

Caleb stared at them a minute.

"Any volunteer to be the next man to hang?" the ranch owner asked them.

Two of the men looked at Norton, but none said a word.

"Cut them loose, Wes. I've made up my mind."

Wes cut their bonds, and then Norton gave them another order they frowned at.

"Now, take off your boots and toss them in a pile."

"What the hell?" one man asked, but Norton couldn't tell which one it was.

Norton stepped down from his horse and pulled out a well-worn Colt, one of the first solid cartridge models they made.

"You men saw Logan hang. You know that the law and the punishment aren't just words anymore. You'll have memories. If any of you ever get the idea to throw a wild rope on some other man's stock, you remember old Roach Logan up there on that rope just twitching and gagging and pissing his pants."

Norton fired a round into the ground in front of the men.

"Get out of here. I never want to see any of your faces again. If I do, I'll yell for the sheriff and charge you with rustling. Git, git. Walk or run, but get the hell out of my sight."

The four men didn't argue about taking a long walk without their boots. It was a lot better than taking a short drop off the hind end of a horse with a noose around your neck.

Wes looked at Norton, seeing him in a new light. Those four men running toward the south and Long Grass would never come anywhere near a rustling operation again.

Norton started to unsaddle his horse.

"Too late to move the cattle today. We'll do it tomorrow. I have two men out rabbit hunting. Let's see what Cookie sent us along for a late-night snack."

An hour later, in the cool darkness, they ate roasted rabbit and hard rolls and jam, brewed coffee and sat around the fire, all wondering how far the rustlers got before they decided it was safe to lie down and go to sleep.

Caleb established a guard for the dark hours. Four men had two-hour shifts. Wes and Slim were not included.

Wes stirred the fire with a stick and looked at his boss. "Mr. Norton, what about Larry Rawls. He has the line shack just below me, doesn't he?"

"Larry is a little on the strange side. Not much of a cowboy, but does a good job as a line rider. Would he sell me out? I don't know. Fact is, after we get our other business done tomorrow, I figured you and Slim and me would pay Larry a surprise visit. Might be interesting."

They went to sleep shortly after that, with their heads on their saddles and their feet toward the fire. For the first time in many nights, Wes felt safe, figured that nobody was gunning for him and that he didn't have to worry about being shot in his sleep.

They had what was left of the hard rolls for breakfast, and some of Cookie's famous dried fruit and nuts trail mix. It turned out to be mostly dried apples and prunes with a few walnuts thrown in. Somehow it was satisfying.

Norton split his riders, sending four of them to drive the one hundred and twenty-five Bar-N steers back to the ranch. They'd be bunched with the other steers ready for market. He got them off and moving, then looked at the two men he had left and Wes and Slim.

"We're gonna find that pass through the breaks and get these cattle on over to the Slant S. Been a while since I've had a good talk with Zip Swanson. We tangled some in our younger years, but the damn breaks keeps our stock apart now."

They started the hundred odd Slash S steers west along the breaks, which rapidly turned to the southwest. Less than two miles along, Norton grinned and pointed to a white bluff that stood out from the rest of the dull brownish hills.

"Right in there we have the passage. Can't get more than two horses or cattle wide through it, but with time we'll get all of these animals stuffed through there. I'll take the lead so I can find a cowboy or somebody to talk to. Wes, you bring up the rear and make sure all them critters get through."

It took them a full two hours to herd the steers through the narrow passage. It had a slight rise to it and then went down on the far side. By noon, they had the stock bunched on the far side of the breaks. Far off in the haze, they could see smoke and some buildings.

"Might as well drive them right up to the barn," Norton said. It took them another two hours to get the steers across the prairie. Caleb rode on ahead, and soon he returned with three men and an older gentleman in a white hat who looked a little unsteady on his horse.

They met and reined to a stop.

Norton introduced Wes and Slim to Zip Swanson, owner of the Slash S.

"I talked Zip's ear off on the way out. His men will take over the steers. He'll vent the trail brand and have no trouble at the railhead.

"We talked about Tom. He's glad now that he knows what happened to him. He figured foul play, but couldn't tell."

"I got to know Tom well in the few days he and I worked together, Mr. Swanson," Wes said. "I'm sorry about the horse. His had a stone bruise, and he wanted to get home and patch up your quarrel. We did catch the men who

234

killed him, and they're all in their own graves now."

Swanson wiped his eyes and nodded. "It's good to have fine neighbors. We need to talk more often." He thanked them all, shook hands with Norton and turned, following his men who drove the steers on ahead.

The four riders headed back toward the breaks and the passageway.

Once on the other side, Norton stopped and looked over the land.

"More west and then south," he said. "Maybe five more miles. We're all going to visit Larry Rawls."

Rawls turned out to be about forty, small and wiry. He had black hair that hadn't been cut for a long time, and a scraggly black beard. His dog growled when the riders came in front of the line cabin.

He looked up and saw Norton, and he scowled.

"Got to be trouble if the boss is way out here," he said.

Norton got down, and the other men dismounted and took their horses for a drink. Wes stayed with Norton.

"Fact is, we did have some trouble up the line a ways. Turned out Roach Logan got himself hanged for cattle rustling."

Rawls made a stab for the six-gun on his hip, but Wes had already drawn his iron and fired a round past Rawls' chest into the front door of the cabin.

"Ease it back home, Rawls," Norton said. "I wouldn't want to have to bury another man today."

"Don't know what you're talking about," Rawls protested. "Thought I saw a coyote over there."

Wes took the iron from Rawls' holster.

"Took me awhile to figure how Logan got the beef to market. Then I remembered how you and him were good friends before you come up here to take Thirteen. Fact is, he suggested you for the job. Said you'd do well up here.

"Never could figure how you didn't need to work during the winter months. You were always on hand for the spring and the trip up to the line shack. Must have taken in more than the two hundred Logan paid the cowboys to help him with the stock. All you had to do was ride to the other side of the range when you saw Logan coming through with his drive to Long Grass. How much did he pay you, Rawls?"

"You can't prove a damn thing, Norton. You know it, and I know it. Why don't I go inside and pack my personal gear, and me and my dog will ride out of here."

Norton nodded. "You do that. Only you don't ride, you walk. That horse out there has a Bar-N brand on it. And don't plan on working anywhere else in the Territory. We got a circulating letter that goes around to the ranches. You'll be at the top of the first sheet telling the other ranchers what a two-timing little bastard you really are."

Anger flared in Rawls' face, then he laughed. "Sure, go ahead and do whatever you want to. I'll be in Omaha where I have my bank account."

They went inside with Rawls so he couldn't pull a rifle on them. He threw some gear and clothes into a bag. Norton checked it to be sure it didn't have a weapon in it, then they pointed him south and watched him walk away with his dog by his side.

Norton scratched his head. "Leaves me with a bit of a problem here. I've got no line rider on Thirteen."

Wes nodded at Slim. His eyes widened.

"Yeah, Mr. Norton, I can do it. Wes here can show me what I don't know. I can do a good job for you."

Caleb Norton chuckled. "Yep, Slim, I bet you can. We'll give you a try. I'll leave one hand here with you for a couple of days to show you the limits of your range. He can bring back a list of food and supplies that you need."

Norton took off his wide-brimmed brown Stetson and reseated it. "Looks like most of our work out here is over. Right now we're about ten miles closer to the Bar-N home place than to Line Shack Twelve. Wes, you might as well ride back with us. We can move along and should get in there sometime around nine or ten o'clock if we don't run up against any trouble."

"Figure we've seen most of the trouble we're gonna for some time now," Wes said.

The three of them headed out after a quick snack from the line shack supplies. They still had a twenty-mile ride.

The three arrived trail weary but pleased a little after ten that night, and Wes fell into an empty bed in the bunkhouse, asleep before he could get his boots off.

The next morning breakfast was huge, and Wes figured he ate at least half of everything served.

Wes and the cook were working up a list of things for him to take back to his shack, when Mr. Norton came in and suggested that they go to town.

Wes asked when, and Norton said in an hour or so.

"Between now and then, you might want to visit Old Jed. He talks about you from time to time."

Wes found the old cowboy in the sitting room. He had a homemade shawl over his legs. His color was good, but when he turned and looked at Wes, his eyes didn't seem to have the same old snap.

"Boy, good to see you again. Hear you had a lot of action out there around Twelve. Looks like I left just at the wrong time. Roach Logan. Damn. I never would have thought it. Just goes to prove you can't tell a man by what he says to you. Got to dig in deeper."

Wes challenged Jed to a game of checkers, but they never got it finished. Jed wanted to talk.

"Don't rightly know what I'm doing here,

sponging off my friend, Mr. Norton. He even pays me ten dollars a month and buys me smokes and peppermint candy. I don't know. I'm about as worthless as a three-legged hound dog trying to swim through a lake filled with alligators."

"Not a chance, Jed. You earned a rest. Just relax and enjoy watching sunsets and the dew on the morning grass. Lots of things out there in this old world besides line shacks and range cattle."

"That's what my daughter Eliza tells me. She wants me to come to Ohio and live with her and her husband. Says they're well fixed, and I wouldn't put them out none. Nonsense and rubbish. An old galoot of a cowboy like me would stick in their craw from the day I opened the door. I don't want to be a charity case to nobody. Course, not much I can do about it right now, but I got me some plans."

Caleb Norton came then and said they had to go to town to report to the sheriff what happened.

Jed waved and said he was almost nigh near to being short on peppermint candies.

Norton nodded and said he'd see what he could do about that.

On the ride into town, fifteen miles away, Norton told Wes that he wanted him along to give the sheriff the whole story about the rustling.

He grinned. "Then, too, the sheriff said he just might have a surprise for you. That's all I can say right now."

In town they stopped first for dinner at a cafe, and Wes put away a steak and all the side dishes. He felt fat and full when they went into the sheriff's office. The sheriff brought in a young deputy to write down what the two ranch men had to say.

Norton talked first, telling about the capture and hanging of Roach Logan. The sheriff looked up, surprised.

"But, I thought he'd been your ramrod out there for nine or ten years."

"He had. That's why it hurt so much to find out he was the one behind the rustling."

Wes took over and retold the whole story of the rustling from the first shooting of Old Jed, and how they finally trapped Logan into trying to run.

With that out of the way, the sheriff took out some papers from his desk and pushed one over to Wes but kept the bottom half of it covered.

"Does that drawing look familiar?"

It was a picture of an outlaw on a wanted poster, and Wes studied the drawing. It wasn't a photo, just a line drawing, but Wes nodded.

"Yes, I just saw him once and then not for long. He said his name was Liberty. J. L. Liberty, something like that. He's the man I killed who had the twenty thousand dollars of the bank's money."

"Which you turned in, correct?"

"Yes, sir."

"You'll swear that this man, J. L. Liberty, is now dead."

"Oh, yes. I had to shoot first, or I'd be the one dead. I didn't want that."

The sheriff moved his hand from the rest of the poster. It showed the man's name as Josh L. Liberty. He was wanted in three states for bank robbery and murder. A bank in Cheyenne had an offer of a two thousand dollar reward for Liberty, dead or alive."

Wes frowned. "He's dead all right. I can take you out and try to find his remains. I kept his wallet and some letters. I think they're out at the ranch.

The sheriff nodded. "No, that won't be necessary. Caleb said that you killed him, and that's good enough for me. I'll fill out the papers and send a wire to Cheyenne today. That two thousand dollars should be yours within a week."

Wes shook his head in surprise. "Just doing what I had to do, that's all."

The sheriff handed Norton a form to look over.

"Like we spoke about a few minutes ago, this is a legal attachment of the funds in the bank account of Roach Logan. He admitted rustling cattle from you and leaving some of the money in the bank. This authorizes you to withdraw some or all of the funds for use in whatever manner you wish."

Norton grinned, filled out the places the sheriff pointed at and tucked the paper in his shirt pocket.

Ten minutes later, they talked to the banker,

who studied the form for a minute, then nodded.

"Yep, now it figures. Never did believe
Roach's story about a rich uncle dying back East.
How do you want the money, cash or a bank
draft?"

"How much is there?" Norton asked.

The banker brought back a ledger and showed
an account page.

"Right now there is seven thousand, seven
hundred and thirty-five dollars and twenty-five
cents."

"Make it two hundred in cash, twenty-dollar
bank notes, and the rest in a cashier's check
made out to Jed Lithrow."

Sixteen

Wes grinned when he heard who the cashier's check was being made out to. He looked at Caleb Norton.

"You're a soft-hearted man, Mr. Norton."

"I've known Jed Lithrow for almost twenty years. He taught me a lot about raising cattle and about being a man a long time ago. It's only right I give him back something."

"But will he take the money?"

"Of course. It's from Roach Logan's account, not mine. You have to help me convince him this is what's best for him."

"Be hard to talk him into that."

"I'm sure you can do it, Wes. You have all the rest of the afternoon and evening."

Back at the Bar-N ranch, Wes and Old Jed played a game of checkers. Jed won, setting up a three-king jump that ended it in a hurry.

"Heard from your daughter lately?" Wes asked.

Jed looked up, a frown warning Wes, but he had to press ahead.

"Yeah, letter last week."

"She asked you to come and stay with them?"

"Does every letter, why?"

"I think you should go. The winters aren't so hard down there in Ohio. Be nice to be with family."

"Putting me out to pasture, right?"

"Like I said before, folks in the city retire after they work thirty, forty years. No reason you can't, too. You've earned it."

"Sponging off relatives. No thanks."

"I'd say you could more than pay your way. Might even be able to help them get a new house if they wanted one."

"Sure, I got piles of cash laying all around. All I have to do is pick it up."

Wes grinned, then laughed softly. "Jed Lithrow, I'd say that's about the case. Pick up that piece of paper." Wes put the cashier's check on the checkerboard.

Jed looked at it a minute. "It's one of them bank drafts."

"Look at it."

Jed turned it around with one finger and picked it up, then held it out at arm's length.

"Be damned, looks like it's got my name on it."

"Sure as hell does, Jed. It says pay to the order of and then there's your name, Jed Lithrow."

"Who would pay an old fart like me anything? Must be a mistake."

"Does it look like a mistake?"

"Can't rightly say. Old eyes ain't as sharp as

244

they used to be. Damn, still can't believe that Roach Logan was behind all that rustling. Just never can tell who to trust these days, can you?"

"Can you read the amount of the check that's made out to you, Jed?"

"Course not. Them little bitty figures. Why don't people write in normal-sized letters and numbers the way they used to so a person can read them?"

Wes took from his pocket the ten twenty-dollar federal bank notes and spread them across the checkerboard.

"I bet you can tell what these are, Jed."

"Hell, yes. Twenty-dollar bills. Any fool can see that. Looks like you struck it rich, boy."

"Not me, Jed. These are yours. Just part of your retirement."

"Retirement? That's when old fogies like me sit around and waste time, and talk an arm and a saddle off whoever they can find, and then worry about how to get to sleep at nights."

Wes chuckled. "Some probably do, but doubt if that's the way you're working it. Not with the money you have."

"What do you mean, money?"

"You haven't seen what those little bitty figures on your retirement check say."

"Wait till I get my magnifying glass. Comes in handy a time or two." He pulled a glass from his sweater pocket and held it over the check. He read the figures mouthing them as he went. He stopped, rubbed his eyes and read them again.

"Can't be right. Says over seven thousand dollars. What the hell you do, rob another bank somewhere?"

"Fact is, we did. You remember that Logan has been rustling cattle off the ranch for five years. He's been spending the money almost as fast as he steals it. This time there was over seven thousand dollars in his bank account.

"The sheriff seized it as illegal profits from the rustling and turned it over to me as a reward for catching the rustlers. Said I could do anything I wanted to with it. I got no use for that much cash money. So I figured you should have it."

"Hell, no! Ain't my money. Belongs to the man it was stole from, our boss, Caleb Norton."

"Mr. Norton thought you'd say that. He said maybe in strict thinking it could be his. But he didn't miss it then, and he won't miss it now. Says that you're more than welcome to it as your retirement pay.

"You said you'd go and live with your daughter if you could walk in with cash money in your fist. Now you can. Wouldn't it be great to be back with your family? I hear you've got a brother and a sister in Ohio and about ten nephews and nieces. Be good to get them all together for a family picnic. Hell, you can pay for everything."

Old Jed sat there thinking a minute.

"Yeah, would be nice to see all the new kids and the kin and all, but ain't my money."

"It is too your money. Fact is, if you don't take

246

it, that banker in town will get to keep it all, and none of us want that, do we?"

"How he get it?"

"Well, it's all in his bank. He wrote this cashier's check. If you don't cash the check and take out the money, it sits right there in his bank under his control for maybe a hundred years, earning interest and making money for the banker and his kids and grandkids. I figure that rich town banker got enough money of his own."

"Fer damn sure."

They sat there, and Wes watched the old man thinking. Longer Wes could keep him thinking, the better. Silence could be a golden weapon sometimes.

Old Jed looked up at Wes. There were tears in his eyes. He tried to brush them away. The back of Jed's hand seemed to have withered some since Jed had noticed. It had brown liver spots on the pale white skin.

"Lord a'mighty. Never seen that much money in all my life. Fact is, don't think I earned that much money all together in my whole life. Just been a cowboy bum, fiddle-footing around. Wouldn't know what the hell to do with all that money."

"Put it in a bank in Ohio and draw it out a little at a time and do whatever you want with it. Take a trip to New York City. Go out to San Francisco and see all those pretty sights. Do anything you want to.

"It'll earn interest, you know. Should earn

four percent. That means on seven thousand dollars, it would earn two hundred and eighty dollars a year. That's twenty-five dollars a month you make just sitting there."

"Oh, damn. I don't know what to do. Be nice to see the family again."

"I checked at the railroad station before we rode home. You can pick up a train any day at noon. That's when the feeder rail line turns around and heads back toward the main line down on the Union Pacific. Take a day and a half, maybe two days on the rails and you'd be in Ohio. A ticket costs only fifty-two dollars. That won't even make a dent in your poke."

Old Jed let the tears come then. He sat there in the rocking chair beside the checkerboard and looked at Wes and cried. He didn't try to stop the flow. Slowly he picked up the ten twenty-dollar bills from the table and folded them and held them tight with both hands.

"Lordy, lordy, lordy. I never thought I'd be going back to see the family. I figured on dropping over dead out here on the plains somewhere. Not yet of course, but some day. Now for sure, I'm going home."

He looked out the window and across the prairie at the distant horizon. "Lordy, I better give Caleb my two week's notice that I'm leaving his employment. Always been a rule of mine, never to just up and quit with no notice."

Wes looked over where Caleb Norton had been standing, just beyond the door, listening.

"I think he'll understand. Why don't I go see if I can find him."

Old Jed nodded and clutched the two hundred dollars tightly to his chest. "I can get up and go. I ain't that crippled up. Walk right good usual in the mornings. What time is it, anyhow, Wesley?"

"Long about six in the evening, Jed."

The dinner bell sounded, and Old Jed put down the checkerboard and lifted the shawl off his legs. "Best be getting out to the feed trough. Boss don't like the hired hands to be late to the table."

Wes nodded at Caleb Norton as he hurried past the ranch owner and out to the mess hall. He wanted one more good meal before he headed up to the high lonely. Oh, he'd take along all the food he could muster. But he didn't want things to spoil. Leastwise this way he could have bacon every morning for nigh onto a week.

Wes smiled at the way Old Jed had come around to deciding to go back home. His mind was made up. Caleb would see him on the train and give the conductors a ten-dollar tip to make sure the old gentleman got onto the east-bound mainliner. Caleb would telegraph Old Jed's daughter that he was coming, and they'd meet him at the train in Columbus, Wes thought it was. Yes, it had been a good day's work.

The next morning, Wes had his horse saddled and a packhorse on a lead line, when Caleb came out of the barn carrying something. Looked like a gunny sack with holes in it. Closer he came, the more curious Wes became.

Caleb had a grin on his face a longhorn wide. He stopped in front of Jed and lifted his arms. The gunny sack fell away, and Jed saw a brown fur ball with big brown eyes and tall, pointy ears.

"Jenny had a litter of pups about six weeks ago. Figure this little male might like a new home about now. That is, if you want to share your food up on Twelve with him. He won't eat much right away. You might even teach him to run down rabbits for both of you to chaw on."

Wes sat there too stunned to do more than give a sheepish grin and try to figure out where to put his hands.

Caleb turned. "Well, if you don't want him. . . ."

Wes yelped and grabbed at the puppy. The sack had been cut so the dog could sit in it, and his head and front paws poked through a hole. The top of the sack had been shortened, and a hole cut so it could hang from the saddle horn.

Wes held up the puppy, got his face licked and the little guy gave a short yip.

"Grow to be a big dog like his ma," Caleb said. " 'Course, if you don't want him. . . ."

Wes hugged the little guy. He was already nearly a foot long, and his eyes had lost their blue shade and were merging to brown. The puppy licked his face, rested a small paw on

Wes's cheek and stared at him with his big, browning eyes. Wes nodded.

"Guess I could keep him, see'n you got too many dogs down here anyway."

Caleb nodded. "Good. Now I only have four more to give away. Maybe if I took them to town."

"Old Jed set for tomorrow?"

"Everything's arranged. Thanks for talking to him yesterday. Somehow you worked it just right."

"Part of my job as a line rider."

"How's the leg?"

"The doc yesterday said Slim did a good job of digging out the lead. He put some new salve on it. All of my cuts and scrapes and holes are healing nicely. Be good as new again in a week or two."

"Good. This time it should really be two months before we see you again. I think you've swept the prairie clear of outlaws up there for a time. You ride back down in sixty days. I want to see how much my puppy there has grown. You thought of a name?"

"You bet. Knew it the minute I saw him. Gonna call him Old Jed."

"Sounds about right."

They both were silent for a minute.

"Want to thank you again for all the risks you took up there on Twelve for the ranch. I appreciate it. You won't be a line rider all your life. Gonna need a new foreman one of these days. Next time I get a permanent foreman, I want to find a man I can trust.

"Now get out of here before your bacon turns rancid. Take care of that puppy."

Wes rode past the front porch where Jed sat in a rocker. Wes got down and showed the puppy to the old man. Jed was delighted to hold the squirming ball of brown fur and feel the big wet tongue across his cheek.

"I'm gonna call him Jed," Wes said, watching the old man beside him.

Tears welled in the old eyes but somehow didn't run over.

"Pleased to hear that. You write me a letter now and then, Wesley. I want to keep up on the ranch doings. I know Caleb won't write. You keep in touch, now, you hear?"

"I'll do that, Jed. Truly I will." He gave Old Jed a man-sized hug, then stepped into the saddle. Old Jed was beside him, handing up the pup. Wes settled him in his bag on the saddle horn, and Old Jed laughed.

They waved and Wes turned his bay into the gentle north breeze and rode toward Line Shack Twelve. He'd spend the rest of the summer and fall up there, then be down with Old Jed, his mostly grown-up dog, for the winter. He had no idea what assignment Caleb Norton would have for him next spring, but whatever it was, he'd do it. He decided he'd found a ranch where he wanted to put in a lot of years.

Wes tickled the brown fur ball under the chin. "Come on, little Jed. Up at Line Shack Twelve I've got a young friend I want to introduce you to. His name is Frisky, and I think you'll like him."

Wes kicked the bay into a gentle trot, and the packhorse followed. Wes Parker was in a hurry now to get home to Line Shack Twelve.

*FOR THE BEST OF THE WEST, SADDLE UP WITH
PINNACLE AND JACK CUMMINGS . . .*

DEAD MAN'S MEDAL   (664-0, $3.50/$4.50)

THE DESERTER TROOP   (715-9, $3.50/$4.50)

ESCAPE FROM YUMA   (697-7, $3.50/$4.50)

ONCE A LEGEND   (650-0, $3.50/$4.50)

REBELS WEST   (525-3, $3.50/$4.50)

THE ROUGH RIDER   (481-8, $3.50/$4.50)

THE SURROGATE GUN   (607-1, $3.50/$4.50)

TIGER BUTTE   (583-0, $3.50/$4.50)

WALK ALONG THE BRINK OF FURY:

THE EDGE SERIES

Westerns By GEORGE G. GILMAN